"You're not my type."

"James continued. "I was married to a career woman like yourself. I have firsthand experience of the genre."

"The genre?" Ellie looked at him in disbelief. "You make it sound as though all women who hold down a job are despicable. This is the twentieth century, just in case you hadn't realized! There's nothing wrong with a woman wanting to achieve something with her life."

"Absolutely not."

"Anyway, has it occurred to you that you're no more my type than I'm yours? I've had firsthand experience of a man like you, and it left a lot to be desired."

"Really?" He sat forward slightly, and Ellie could have kicked herself for the slipup.

CATHY WILLIAMS is Trinidadian and was brought up on the twin islands of Trinidad and Tobago. She was awarded a scholarship to study in Britain, and came to Exeter University in 1975 to continue her studies into the great loves of her life: languages and literature. It was there that Cathy met her husband, Richard. Since they married, Cathy has lived in England, originally in the Thames Valley but now in the Midlands. Cathy and Richard have three small daughters.

Books by Cathy Williams

HARLEQUIN PRESENTS®
2222—MERGER BY MATRIMONY
2184—A SCANDALOUS ENGAGEMENT
2165—THE BABY SCANDAL

Don't miss any of our special offers. Write to us at the following address for information on our newest releases.

Harlequin Reader Service
U.S.: 3010 Walden Ave., P.O. Box 1325, Buffalo, NY 14269
Canadian: P.O. Box 609, Fort Erie, Ont. L2A 5X3

Cathy Williams

WILLING TO WED

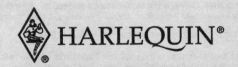

HARLEQUIN®

TORONTO • NEW YORK • LONDON
AMSTERDAM • PARIS • SYDNEY • HAMBURG
STOCKHOLM • ATHENS • TOKYO • MILAN • MADRID
PRAGUE • WARSAW • BUDAPEST • AUCKLAND

ISBN 0-373-18774-2

WILLING TO WED

First North American Publication 2002.

Copyright © 1997 by Cathy Williams.

This edition published by arrangement with Harlequin Books S.A.

® and TM are trademarks of the publisher. Trademarks indicated with
® are registered in the United States Patent and Trademark Office, the
Canadian Trade Marks Office and in other countries.

Visit us at www.eHarlequin.com

Printed in U.S.A.

CHAPTER ONE

It was after ten-thirty that evening when Ellie stepped into her flat—the earliest she had been there for weeks, bar the occasional day off when the unexpected break from work had almost had her feeling lost and purposeless. She had become so accustomed to her constant state of overdrive that total relaxation now seemed a thing of the past, something that other people indulged in—people who also had time to do things like watch television, take walks, read a book cover to cover in under six months.

Being prominent in the field of medicine required a way of thinking that viewed sleep as something to be done only when absolutely necessary, and even then always with one ear ready and alert for the sound of a bleeper, or the telephone ringing, heralding some emergency that couldn't wait.

There were three pieces of mail on the carpet. Ellie automatically picked them up without looking at them, taking off her jacket and switching on the answering machine, which she listened to while she poured herself a glass of juice.

Four messages. Two friends who wanted to find out whether she was still alive. Harrods informing her that the coat she had ordered had now arrived. And Henry, asking her whether supper on Saturday was still on. Henry, Henry, Henry. She sighed and gulped back her juice, then rubbed her eyes and wondered what it would be like to sleep for forty days and forty nights, without interruption.

She was only thirty-four, unmarried, and it occasionally crossed her mind that most women of her age, without family ties, would be out enjoying themselves, going to jobs which they could leave behind at civilised hours so that they had enough time to socialise.

There's no gain without pain, she told herself, staring out of the darkened kitchen into the charmingly furnished sitting room. I have a thoroughly enjoyable if demanding job and I have freedom. The freedom of not having to depend on anyone for anything. And I'm not lonely, because I have dear Henry.

She walked into the bathroom and turned on both bath taps. She pulled her hair free—blonde, straight hair that fell down her back, almost to her waist. It took years off her and she knew that, which was why she never ventured near the hospital without it being pinned up severely. Looking younger than their age might be desirable for other women, but it was a drawback in her profession. Patients were suspicious of doctors who did not look old enough. Age, most of them assumed, accompanied experience and it would have been impossible to explain that, although that might be true enough, experience did not always accompany competence.

It was only when she had stepped out of her shoes and switched off the bath that she remembered the post. The first two she scanned. Both bills, one a second reminder, which would have to be sorted out some time over the weekend. The third one, in a heavy cream envelope, made her stop. She turned it over curiously, looking for clues, then she removed her clothes and stepped into the bath, enjoying the contemplation of trying to work out who the letter was from. A childish game which, after a grim, busy day at the hospital, was strangely relaxing.

It was with some reluctance that she finally slit it open, to find a short note which she read quickly at first, then more slowly and with growing disbelief and alarm.

It took her several seconds to digest the information. Her father was seriously ill. A stroke. Quite sudden. Recovering satisfactorily, but her presence, the person who had penned the note had written, with a sarcasm which was implied rather than stated, might not be such a bad idea.

She squinted at the signature and gradually placed a face to the name.

James Kellern. His father had owned the huge estate next to her father's far more modest plot of land. She distantly recalled a dark-haired young man whom she had seen on and off during her school holidays, when she had returned from boarding-school and had had nothing better to do than read and take walks. A rather unfriendly young man, she remembered. His father had been a friend and patient of her father, as had nearly all of the people living in the Irish village where, as the one and only GP, Dr Mills had had the monopoly on dispensing medicines and words of advice.

Ellie had only formally been introduced to James Kellern once and the occasion had left a lot to be desired. She had been a teenager at the time and, although only a matter of four or five years older than her, he had seemed frighteningly worldly-wise and condescending.

She dried herself hurriedly, and without pausing to think the matter through she telephoned the number on the headed notepaper.

It was already after eleven but she didn't give a damn. It only rang once before it was answered, and Ellie, with automatic courtesy, said, 'I do apologise for calling at this hour, but I wonder if I might speak to Mr James Kellern, please?'

She rested back against the bedhead and stared straight ahead of her, across the semi-lit room into the mirror opposite the bed, absent-mindedly watching the reflection staring back at her. A shadowy reflection, but she could fill in the blurry pieces. The green eyes, fringed with thick, dark eyelashes, the small, straight nose, the well-shaped mouth. A face that could be sexy but for the look of efficient self-control which had become part and parcel of her nature.

As she had climbed up the medical ladder, her brains and dedication silencing first the nudge-nudge grins of her male contemporaries, then their scepticism, Ellie had lost touch with that element of feminine vanity that could turn a pleasing face into an irresistible one.

'Why?'

'Excuse me?' That made her sit up a bit more. The voice that reached her from the other end was deeper, more forceful and infinitely more bad-tempered than she had anticipated. Even at a little after eleven at night.

'I asked why? Who, first of all, is it, and what, secondly, do you want?'

'Get me James Kellern, please. At once!'

There was a brief silence down the line, then the deep, forceful voice returned, this time cool and cautious.

'Miss Mills. Or should I say Ms? I recognise the voice of a woman in a position of influence. Ms Mills, this is James Kellern and I assume that you've received my letter.'

Ellie pulled her dressing gown around her, uneasily feeling that if she blinked hard enough the owner of that voice would suddenly be standing in front of her.

'That's right,' she answered crisply. 'How is my father? May I talk to him?'

'Your father is doing as well as can be expected, and no, you may not talk to him because he's asleep. I assume you're aware of the hour?'

'What exactly happened and why was I not notified at the time?'

'Your father collapsed four weeks ago and—'

'Four weeks! And this is the first I've heard of it!'

There was anger and shock in her voice, and a certain amount of guilt which she hoped was not discernible to him. Her relationship with her father was strained at the best of times, and over the last few months—or was it years?—it had petered out into a formal exchange of cards at appropriate times, the occasional phone call and the odd visit, although, when she came to think of it, she couldn't quite remember when she had last gone over to Ireland.

She bit her lip and felt a sudden pang of remorse, which was swiftly followed by memories of why she had avoided her family home: the gut-wrenching nervousness which started the minute she arrived and didn't go away until she left, the loneliness, the miserable knowledge that she, an only child, was a disappointment to her father.

'He insisted that everything was fine and that there was no need to contact you.'

'I see,' Ellie said stiffly. 'And no one, including yourself, stopped to consider that I am his daughter, and that I might be just a little concerned about my father's health?'

'Frankly, no.' There was a pause. 'He was quite adamant, Ms Mills, and I saw no reason to go against his wishes. It's hardly as though you've been a frequent visitor to these parts. Apparently the last time you came over here was in the region of two and a half years ago. For a weekend.'

So now you're passing judgement on me, she thought with a sudden flare of resentment. Her skin was burning and, much as she would have liked to defend herself, there really was no point.

'Does he know that you've contacted me now?' she asked, changing the subject and trying to inject an element of calm into her voice.

'No.' There was another pause and she got the feeling

that he was trying to work out what to say next. 'I felt I had to, however. Your father's condition has raised certain issues which need to be sorted out.'

'Issues? What do you mean, *issues*? What kind of issues?'

'Better discussed face to face, I think,' the voice informed her flatly. 'When can you get here?'

Ellie's brain worked rapidly, sifting through details of what she had to do over the next fortnight, which patients needed careful, personal monitoring, what courses she was due to attend.

'You *can* get over here some time in the foreseeable future, I take it?' His voice was several shades cooler and she could imagine what he was thinking. Ms High-Powered Mills, all hot under the collar at the thought of not having been notified about her father, but suddenly hesitant about committing herself to a date to see him. He wouldn't understand that it simply boiled down to rearranging things, a matter that couldn't be decided in a split second down the end of a telephone.

'Naturally I can get over there, Mr Kellern,' she replied coldly.

'Glad to hear it.' He sounded unimpressed. 'In that case, what about this Saturday?'

He had, she noticed, a way of voicing questions which seemed to brook no argument with him. Where had he acquired that? She tried to remember what he had done with his life, but she couldn't. Her participation in life in her home town had been minimal and her father quite simply did not communicate by way of chatty, informative letters. He was not a chatty, informative *man*. At least not with her.

'I'm afraid...'

'Listen to me, Ms Mills,' he said in a low, cutting voice. 'Your father needs you. I suggest you find a way to make it over here on Saturday. If you leave early enough in the morning, you can be here by mid-afternoon. I will arrange for a car to meet you at the airport.'

'Saturday is only two days away! I may need a little more time to rearrange all my commitments...'

He had obviously consulted a timetable while she had been talking, because his next words were to inform her of exactly when on Saturday she would be leaving, and what time she would be arriving at the airport.

'You'll be expected,' he told her. Then he hung up.

Just like that! He hung up! She couldn't believe it! She remained with the receiver in her hand for a few seconds, incredulous. She was highly respected in her field; her advice was sought and listened to. It had been a while since she had found herself on the defensive with anyone, and the experience confused and angered her.

Had she become so used to giving orders that she found it difficult to tolerate the tendency in someone else? She switched off the side-light and frowned. It wasn't in her nature to delve too heavily into the emotional side of herself. Her schedule did not allow her the luxury of too much self-analysis.

Now her subconscious stirred into life, making up for that, throwing images of herself back at her, then sifting back through the past to remind her of distant days. Her relationship with her father was rooted in pride, stubbornness and silences that eventually couldn't be penetrated.

Even now, she could still feel that bewilderment and pain which had accompanied her through childhood. The lack of physical affection, the gradual realisation that whatever she had to offer her father it simply wasn't enough and never would be. That awful, overheard conversation, listening outside the kitchen door, eight or nine years old and nervously aware that she'd be killed if she got caught. Gladys, the cleaner at the time, and the cook cosily chatting about poor little Eleanor, if only her mother hadn't died in childbirth, leaving Dr Mills with the legacy of a dead wife and to show for it a girl when everyone knew that he had wanted a son. A son to carry on the family name. Things might have been different...but that poor child, well, she just couldn't put a foot right, could she?

Thirty-four years old, a grown woman, and the memories still hurt.

By the time Thursday dawned, those memories had slipped back into the box where they belonged. There was no place for them in the present, no room for morbid introspection. Ellie was just too busy, and the little time she had to herself she filled madly with making arrangements so that she could get away on Saturday.

She had no idea how long she would be away, but she couldn't see it being longer than a week at the most, especially since, from what she had been told, her father was out of danger and really just recuperating now.

The most difficult call, which theoretically should have been the easiest, turned out to be the call to Henry. Maybe she had sensed that, deep down, because it was Friday night before she phoned him, and shortly before she was ready for bed...

Henry had, she reflected now as she stared out of the aeroplane window, not been amused. He had been suitably sympathetic, but there had been grudging complaint in his voice.

'I haven't seen you in two weeks!' he had protested. 'This was to be our first Saturday out in God knows how long!'

As if she could alter circumstances accordingly. For the umpteenth time she had thought, fleetingly, how little understanding Henry had of her circumstances. He was a doctor as well, but a general practitioner, and his hours were therefore far more controllable. He could plan things ahead, fairly secure in the knowledge that his plans would materialise and not be blown out of the water by some unexpected emergency. It frequently surprised Ellie that although he was in the same profession as she was, so should be able to sympathise with her situation, Henry still became sulky when her hours conflicted with time planned for them to spend together.

'I could always come with you,' he had suggested, and that had been another sticky matter of dissuading him from the idea.

The fact was, she was too uncompromising to have a boyfriend, too hell-bent on pursuing her career. At least at this present moment in time. Henry would have to be patient. She didn't let herself think about what she would do if he wasn't. She liked him very much. She guessed she loved him, in a pleasant, easy way. She would miss him dreadfully if he weren't around.

It felt odd to be sitting here, with time to think. Gradually, as the desire to fidget faded, she relaxed. What would she do when she arrived home? She couldn't imagine her father as anything but invulnerable. Would he be even colder and more cantankerous because he might have to look to her for help occasionally? The thought dismayed her and she immediately felt even more guilty at her increasing lack of filial duty over the years, at that little part of her that viewed the next few days with sickening trepidation. She closed her eyes and tried not to think at all until the plane landed.

Stepping out of the plane and walking towards the airport terminal was like taking a trip back in time and Ellie savoured a bitter-sweet flashback of memories. Memories of arriving back here from boarding-school in Surrey, year after year, until gradually, as she got older, holidays were spent in other places. She'd stayed with friends in other parts of the country and later, when she was at university in Cambridge, had stayed at the university itself, studying most of the time, socialising the rest, with other medical students, most of whom she had now lost touch with.

It was stuffy in the terminal. Outside, it was warm. A glorious spring day holding the tenuous promise of similar days to come.

She was standing scanning the cars outside, looking for the taxi sent to collect her, when a familiar voice spoke from slightly behind her.

'Ms Mills?' The same deep, critical voice that had got on her nerves over the telephone.

She spun around and the mid-afternoon sun caught her in the eye, so that she had to shield her face and stare up at him.

James Kellern. A blurred memory last seen through the eyes of a girl. Now seen through the eyes of a woman. A tall, lean-built man with a face arresting enough to make her momentarily disoriented. A strong, hard-featured face, grey eyes and very dark, almost black hair. It was less the physical detail that struck her, though, and more the impression of forcefulness. What she was seeing now matched the voice perfectly.

'That's right,' she said politely, shifting her eyes away. 'You must be Mr Kellern.' It was strangely disconcerting to focus too hard on such spectacular good looks. She felt that he might find her inspection intrusive, although he must surely be used to women staring at him. It would certainly account for his vast self-assurance.

'I am.' He nodded to his left. 'My car's over there. Can I take your bag?'

'It's all right. I can manage.'

He shrugged and walked towards a green Range Rover while she struggled to keep pace with him and at the same time answer his polite questions about her trip.

'I'll put your bag in the boot, shall I?' he asked, looking at her as she climbed into the passenger seat. 'Or would you rather do that yourself as well?'

'Thank you.' She glanced up at the bent, dark head with sudden dislike. In the early days, she had to put up with a lot of patronising from men. Sheer ability had been the tool which had eventually won her respect. It was a respect which she was not about to forfeit to a virtual stranger who had clearly passed judgement on her and found her wanting.

'How is my father? Really?' she asked, once he was inside the car and they were moving. She watched the hard, chiselled profile, disturbed to find that her long-acquired detachment seemed to have deserted her.

'Much better. Really.' He glanced swiftly across at her. 'His right side's been affected slightly. He finds speaking difficult, he slurs his words, and his control over his right arm and leg is poor, although they've said that will improve in time. Right now, he's finding those physical nuisances hard to accept.'

'I can imagine,' Ellie said, staring through the window. Her father had never suffered from ill health. Now, she imagined, he would be feeling betrayed by his body, intolerant of its shortcomings.

'I've hired someone to look after him,' James informed her. 'A trained nurse, who has a lot of experience in this field.'

'*You've* hired…?'

'That's right.' Have you got an argument with that? his voice seemed to imply.

'Since when have you become close to my father?'

'Do I detect an element of disapproval?'

'You detect nothing of the sort, Mr Kellern…' But he did, loath as she was to admit it. Or maybe it was just good, old-fashioned jealousy that *her* presence had been actively discouraged by her father, whilst the next-door neighbour was honoured with the task of tending him back to health. She shook her head to clear it of the disturbing thought.

'You can call me James. We have, after all, been neighbours all our lives.'

'James, then.' Actually, she preferred Mr Kellern. It maintained a certain distance between them which she had no desire to lessen. Neighbours they might well have been, but only in the most limited sense of the word. She knew more about her postman than she did about the man sitting next to her.

'To be perfectly blunt, Eleanor...'

'Ellie,' she said automatically.

'Ellie.' He looked at her for a split second. Was it her imagination, or was he trying to work out whether the face fitted the name? 'Your father needed someone to look after him when he came out of hospital, and outside help was the only possible solution.'

'Thank you, but I can't help my job,' Ellie said, guiltily aware that those caretaking duties should have fallen on her shoulders, hearing the defensive challenge in her voice and hating herself for it.

'I never implied that you could. I'm simply saying that help was needed and I made sure he got it.'

'In which case, why isn't he at home? Why is he with you?'

'Because,' he explained patiently, 'Mrs Cribb leaves at six in the evening and I didn't think it advisable for your father to be on his own between six in the evening and eight in the morning, which is when she arrives. At least, not at the moment.'

'I see.' She stared out of the window for a while, then said in a more conciliatory voice, 'You still haven't told me how you and my father suddenly became such close friends. He hasn't mentioned you in any of his letters.' She didn't add that that really meant very little, since her father's letters were few and far between and tended to cover topics which were anything but personal. She knew all her father's opinions on the government, the economy, the falling standards of education, medical advances, and virtually nothing about what he thought and felt about himself.

'My father was a close friend of George. When I moved back to manage the estate after my father's death, I carried on the friendship. That,' he added, with a sidelong glance, 'was almost four years ago.'

'Implying...?'

'Implying nothing. Merely responding to your question.'

'Why is it that I get the feeling you're criticising me?'

'I have no idea,' he answered smoothly. 'Perhaps your conscience is working overtime.'

Ellie felt colour creep into her face. What gave this man the right to jump to his own scathing conclusions about her? The little voice whispering in her head that he had a point did nothing to quell her anger.

'I realise that I fall short of your definition of a good daughter...'

'Of most people's definition of a good daughter, actually...'

'...which is regrettable, but I really don't think that we're going to get anywhere by allowing it to be a bone of contention. I know absolutely nothing about you and I have no intention of changing that. I'd very much appreciate it if you would do me the favour of keeping your opinions to yourself. I don't expect you to understand what motivates me and I'm not asking you to try.'

'What *does* motivate you?' he asked curiously. 'I'm interested.'

Like hell you are, she thought with an unnatural surge of aggression. 'Being good at what I do.'

'Paediatric medicine.'

'That's right. Which, incidentally, is why I simply can't find the time to come up to see Father very often. I barely get the time to sit down and have a cup of coffee.'

'And you enjoy the feeling of being constantly rushed off your feet?'

'It's all part of the job.' She looked at him critically, wondering whether he understood that or whether he typically expected women to get married, have babies and remain at home, being the perfect wife, mother and general support network to one and all. Wasn't that how it was with all of these good-looking, debonair, sophisticated types? They felt it their right to forge ahead with their careers, but when it came to women—well, the little things were much better off wearing an apron and tied to a kitchen sink, weren't they?

She hurtled back through time, back to when she was young and foolish, eighteen years old and on the threshold of her future. Back to that brief, catastrophic fling with Cameron Clark—wonderful, charming Cameron Clark, with his fabulous blond looks and his keen brain. And his conviction that she was utterly mad to pursue a career in medicine.

Oh, that was fine for other women, he'd claimed, but not for her, because he envisaged a future for them together and any woman who was part of his future, by definition, didn't hold down a demanding job. What on earth would happen when the time came to start a family? More to the point, how could any woman consider herself useful to a man if she didn't devote all of her time to his needs?

Ellie preferred not to think of Cameron Clark. Indeed, she seldom did. She supposed that something in James Kellern had brought back the memory.

'When was the last time you took a holiday?' she

heard him asking now, and she snapped back to the present.

'Is this a cross-examination?' Somehow, James Kellern managed to put her on the defensive. She felt as though she had to counter-attack questions which, coming from anyone else, would have been little more than polite conversation.

'Why so sensitive?' He shot her a sudden hard, speculative look which she met with tightened lips.

'I am not sensitive. And, as a matter of fact, the last time I took a holiday was...' she frowned and cast her mind back '...a year or so ago. I went to Paris.'

'Charming city. How long were you there?'

'A long weekend.'

He gave a shout of laughter. 'A weekend! What on earth did you manage to see in a weekend? You must have spent the entire time running between places of interest.'

She had, as a matter of fact. She had gone with Henry and it had not been a relaxing experience. 'It was very relaxing, now that you ask,' she lied.

They had left Dublin and the fast lanes of the motorway behind and were now moving rather more slowly along the back roads that led to the Courtney Manor stud farm. Shortly, the road would fork. Left to her father's house. Right, eventually, to Courtney Manor.

'You mentioned on the phone that Father's stroke had raised certain issues that needed to be discussed. Would you mind telling me what they are?'

'All in good time,' James informed her.

'This seems a pretty good time to me,' Ellie said, forcing herself to sound pleasant, though not particularly liking his tone of voice.

'Well, I don't think it's a good time. I think you ought to see your father first. I've told him you're coming.' He turned right and they passed his estate, acres of land, before finally swerving through the open wooden gate and up along the very long lane that led to the Manor.

'Good heavens!' she said, startled. 'It's a thousand times bigger than I remembered!'

'I thought that things became smaller the older one got.' She caught his half-smile of amusement and quashed a sudden, disturbing array of emotions. Underneath that overpowering masculinity, which she found so abrasive, was the glimpse of something dangerously sexy. She averted her eyes quickly back to the Manor, now drawing closer and closer.

It was a vast, sprawling mansion, immaculately maintained thanks to the considerable Kellern family money. Its honey-rust colour was interrupted by climbing ivy and its backdrop of trees was almost as impressive as the front approach. On the odd occasion when she had trundled across with her father to see old Mr Kellern, they had taken a short cut through the estate and approached via a side-entrance, so that the immediate impact of the house had been lost.

The lane gave way to a gravelled courtyard and as the prospect of seeing her father drew nearer Ellie felt that familiar attack of nerves. She could not remember a time when she had faced her father without butterflies in her stomach.

'Does it seem smaller now?' James murmured into her ear, once they were inside the house and the housekeeper had taken her bag upstairs to her room.

Ellie looked around her at the huge hall, with its black and white tiles and series of doors leading off to rooms she could no longer even begin to visualise, and shook her head slowly.

'The opposite, if anything. I feel as though I ought to ask for a map so that I can find my way around.' She faced him with an uncertain expression. 'There's really no need for me to stay here, you know. I could take Father back to the house while I'm here...'

'It would be a pointless disruption. At least it would be at this moment in time.'

This moment in time? Why didn't she like the sound of that?

He turned away and began walking down the corridor, which was wide and hung on both sides with a series of animal paintings, primarily horses, some of which she recognised. 'Your father's waiting for you in the sitting room,' he said over his shoulder. 'I haven't asked whether you want to recover from your flight before meeting him. I assume you don't.'

'You're fond of making assumptions, aren't you, Mr Kellern? I mean James.'

He stopped in his tracks and turned to face her. 'You have a very dictatorial way of talking. Do you know that?' His expression relaxed suddenly and she felt her heart beat a little faster for a few seconds. 'Like a teacher. I almost feel as though I ought to stand to attention. Is it part of the job?'

Ellie looked up at him, stupidly hurt by the remark. It wasn't so much what he'd said, more the way he'd said it. Men, she thought, seldom got under her skin. Time had fortified her defences, made her invulnerable to personal slings and arrows. Yet here she was now, hot and bothered, responding to this man as though what he said and thought really mattered to her.

'I haven't seen evidence of you doing any such thing,' she told him, and he laughed, which made her responses go haywire all over again.

'Are you taking me to see my father?' she asked, folding her arms. 'Or shall we just while away our time with you making personal, sniping remarks at me?'

'Onward we go, m'lady,' he said, moving on. 'Or should I say sir?'

'Very funny,' Ellie muttered under her breath, stung. She wished that she hadn't pinned her hair up again in her usual neat little bun. She wished that she had left it loose. Then he would have seen that she was a woman and not merely a high-ranking doctor with a string of letters after her name. Not, of course, that it mattered. Least of all to a man like this one.

Her father was waiting for them. Ellie saw him before he saw her, because he was staring out of the window, his hands fidgeting on his lap, his mouth downturned, the expression of a man frustrated by his immobility.

Impulsively, she stretched out her hand and placed it on James's arm, stopping him just for a moment so that she could continue to observe her father while she was still unnoticed.

He looked much frailer than she remembered. Less forbidding, more vulnerable, although she still found it nearly impossible to think of him along the lines of someone who was vulnerable. Although it was warm in the room, he was wearing a long-sleeved shirt and a bow tie. He had always been a stickler for formal wear, but nothing could disguise his loss of weight.

She still felt that sickening tightening in her stomach, though. The same old feeling of someone about to enter into combat, except there was never any combat with her father, only the depressing chasm between two people who had become strangers over the years.

She took a deep breath, removed her hand, and said, 'All right. I'm ready.' The words were spoken in a whisper to James, but they were directed at herself. She could feel herself perspiring lightly and she licked her lips.

'Hello, Father.'

The old man turned slowly to look at her. After a lengthy inspection, he nodded unsmilingly.

'Eleanor, my dear. I did tell James that there was no need for you to trouble yourself.'

Ellie sighed and moved into the room to stand next to his chair, dutifully kissing the top of his head.

'I'm so sorry about the stroke, Father.' She sat down in the chair facing his, aware that James had tactfully left the room. 'I wish you'd called me, let me know. I would have come over sooner.'

'Nonsense, my girl.' He looked at her carefully. 'Be back on my feet in no time at all. Really no need for you to have rushed over here. Damned inconvenient for you, I'm sure.'

'Not at all.' Ellie smiled, but inside she could feel her heart sinking. Why was it always this way between them? Two polite strangers talking to one another, not quite finding the right way. Had it ever been different? She could remember the same inspection routine when she was a child, the same question and answer routine, the same lurking suspicion of disapproval behind those assessing, paternal eyes. And every time she told herself that she could cope with it all she would find herself facing him on one of her rare visits, and the hurt would come flooding back all over again.

'Still. Good to see you, whatever the circumstances. Now. Tell me what's happening in London. Read in the newspapers something about that hospital of yours facing closure. What's that all about, my girl?'

'They got the facts wrong.' Ellie sighed and looked out of the window to the immense gardens, dappled by spring sunshine. She wondered whether she would ever know this man sitting opposite her, and whether he would ever know her.

CHAPTER TWO

'HE LOOKS terrible.' Ellie stared across the kitchen table to where James was sitting, finishing his cup of coffee.

Except, he thought, she wasn't really looking at him. She was staring somewhere into infinity and her thoughts were a thousand miles away. Irritatingly, he realised that he would like to climb into her head and unravel what she was thinking. A frustrating feeling, since normally he could not care less what the opposite sex thought of him. He had been through one catastrophic relationship and it had been enough to ensure that his curiosity about women was now restricted to the minimum. He was quite happy to allow nature to take its course in his dealings with them.

He looked at the cool, contained blonde opposite him, frowning now, and said evenly, 'He looks better than he did a few weeks ago. His colour has returned.' He stared at her narrowly, and was gratified when she at least returned the look, though absent-mindedly. 'Why were you so nervous about seeing him?'

'What do you mean?'

This time, she focused on him sharply, and despite the warning in her eyes he felt an insane need to push his way through the coldness and quiz her until he could at least get near to whatever lay behind the controlled exterior.

I must be bored, he told himself. Playing games with a woman who probably only gets excited when she's talking about her career. In a minute, just as soon as this cup of coffee's finished, I'll leave and let the devil work on idle hands somewhere else.

'You made me stop at the door and then you took a deep breath as though you were about to face an ordeal.'

'You have a very active imagination. I simply wanted to look at him, to gauge how badly the stroke had affected him.'

'I see. From a purely medical point of view.'

'Something like that,' Ellie muttered.

He drained his cup of coffee and decided that now was as good a time as any to leave because she was beginning to get on his nerves with her tight-lipped, unresponsive answers. Angrily, he found himself relaxing further back in his chair.

'What a warm, spontaneous response.' He could hear the heavy, uncalled-for sarcasm in his voice and could see that she was as aware of it as he was, because she flushed slightly and threw him a cool, disapproving look.

'Do you think you could see your way to sparing me your opinions?'

'Why? Don't you like other people making personal remarks to you?' When she reddened like that, she looked younger, more vulnerable, and he wondered what she looked like with her hair down, laughing. His eyes skirted away from her face, along the smooth column of her neck, and down to the outline of her breasts pushing against her shirt.

Abruptly he refocused his attention on her face, which was cool and guarded. Precisely the sort of face guaranteed to put him off.

'Does anyone? When an insult is implied?'

'Most people welcome a little healthy criticism.'

'Well, in that case, why don't you try locating those people and then you can lavish all your pearls of wisdom on *them*?'

James's mouth tightened and he had to suppress the temptation to enter into a fully fledged argument with her. Who the hell did she think she was? Any other normal human being would have been bending over backwards in gratitude for what he had done for her father, looking after him when his daughter should have been the one filling the role. But oh, no, not Ms Eleanor Mills. So wrapped up in her busy, demanding job in the city that not even her father had the audacity to turn to her in his hour of need.

He had not intended telling her quite yet why he had contacted her. He had meant to give her at least a night to acclimatise herself to being back in her home town, but her evident dislike of him made any notions of being gradual and gentle in laying down what he had to say fly through the window.

He stood up and pushed back his chair. 'Would you like something a little stronger to drink? There are a few things we need to discuss and we might as well discuss them somewhere a little more comfortable.'

'Oh, yes. These mysterious issues.' She stood up too and even though he kept his eyes on her face he couldn't help but notice the shape of her body underneath her jeans. Slim, almost boyish. A figure to match the small, upright breasts. Nothing overtly sexy there, but something disconcertingly appealing nevertheless. Maybe it was that hint of the woman behind the robot, he thought sarcastically.

He reminded himself that she was not his type at all. Neither in her personality nor in the way she was built. He tended to go for bigger, bustier women. Outgoing women who weren't afraid of flirting or laughing. Women who made few demands on his intellect and were content to play the same light games as he was.

She followed him out of the kitchen and into the sitting room, where he went across to what appeared to be an ornate piece of carved furniture, but which turned out to be a bar.

'Will you join me?' he asked politely, not surprised

when she shook her head. 'Don't tell me you don't touch the stuff?'

He turned around to face her and noticed that she had made sure to sit down on the chair furthest away from the sofa. What did she imagine he was going to do? he wondered. Jump on her for no apparent reason?

'Well?' he persisted. 'Does the occasional drink not feature in your fun-packed calendar at all?'

Ellie glared at him from under her lashes. 'Yes. The occasional drink does feature in my fun-packed calendar. It's quite simply that my calendar is more work-packed at the moment than it is fun-packed and, strange though it may seem, drinking on the wards isn't exactly encouraged.'

'You're not on a ward now,' he pointed out, and she gave an exasperated sigh.

'Are you *always* this persistent? Oh, all right, then. I'll have a…a…whatever it is you're having.'

He poured her a gin and tonic, curiously wondering whether she had ever been the worse for drink. No, of course not, he told himself with a little sneer. That would entail letting her guard down, and he doubted she ever did that, even when totally relaxed.

Which she obviously wasn't now. At least, not to judge by the way she was sitting bolt upright in the chair, legs crossed, fingers linked protectively over one knee.

'Don't you ever play at all?' he found himself asking conversationally, knowing that the question was an unnecessary attempt to goad her into a reaction.

'Issues!' She gulped some of her drink and the colour mounted her cheeks. 'Remember? That's what we're here to talk about.'

'I prefer to lead up to serious topics via the route of pleasantries,' he said, forcing himself to relax and smile. He crossed his legs and surveyed her with what he hoped would project the impression of detached interest. The kind of interest a scientist might reveal in the face of the latest piece of amusingly preposterous medical research. 'After all, I don't know a thing about you, apart from what your father's told me off and on.'

'And what might that be?'

He shrugged and swallowed a little more of his drink. 'Briefly, what you do for a living.' He could see her absorbing this and wondered whether he imagined the fleeting disappointment in her eyes before she gazed at him with a return of her attentive yet detached politeness. 'Funny that we never bumped into one another even though we lived next door, isn't it?'

'There's quite a bit of land separating the two houses,' she said. 'And we were both at boarding-school. It's not really that surprising when you think about it.' She took another little mouthful of her gin and tonic. 'Also, once I got to university, I hardly ever returned here for holidays.' She flushed and then carried on hastily, 'I mean, medicine requires a great deal of dedication. Still does.'

'You know what they say about all work and no play, et cetera, et cetera.'

'Is that right?' Her eyes sparked and, for reasons that he couldn't analyse, that excited him. 'And what do *you* do for play? Managing this estate can't absorb all of your time, surely. What were you doing before you came back here to live?'

There were no overhead lights switched on, merely side-lamps, and the mellow glow from them threw her face into intriguing shadow and light. Her hair, tightly swept up away from her face, elongated the lines of her neck and gave her a fragile appearance. She looked nothing like a doctor—at least none that he had ever had dealings with.

She was looking at him curiously and he finished his drink, suddenly aware that he had flushed under her level gaze.

'Pretty much the same as you were, as a matter of fact,' he answered. 'University—though not medicine, I hasten to add. I never could stand the sight of blood. Economics, followed by a very good career in London.' He looked at her and wondered how much she knew, via her father, about him. Not much, judging from the look on her face. 'Oh, yes, and there was a brief stint at marriage.'

'What?'

That, at any rate, had jolted her out of her self-composure. She looked startled and, much as he wasn't given to holding forth on that particular episode in his life with anyone—least of all someone he had known for five minutes—he heard himself launching into the subject and was vaguely astounded by himself.

'Marriage,' he repeated. When was the last time that word had crossed his lips? He couldn't remember. What was the point of replaying mistakes when learning from them was more constructive? 'I take it you're aware of the institution?'

'My father never mentioned it to me...'

He could see her trying to resurrect some distant memory, but her face remained blank.

'Regrettably, it didn't work out.' His mouth twisted.

'What went wrong?'

'We got married without thinking about it. In retrospect, we hardly knew each other at all. We were both in high-powered careers, in the thick of London, enjoying the rich lifestyle of the unencumbered. What could make more sense than marriage?'

'Obviously quite a bit,' Ellie said dryly.

'It was only once we were married that certain major rifts began appearing. They culminated in my father's death, when I decided to return here and get the place back into working order. Antonia couldn't stand the country lifestyle.' He hated talking about it, but he found that he couldn't stop. He could see his ex-wife's beautiful, dissatisfied face as clearly as if she were standing in the room in front of him, could hear her angry, harsh voice informing him that she had no intention of burying herself in rustic domesticity, that she'd rather commute between Dublin and London than accept that. He remembered, as if it were yesterday, the arguments which all ended in doors being slammed before any conclusion or compromise could be reached between them.

'Shortly after I came up here, she told me that she was pregnant, but despite an unstable pregnancy she continued to lead her hectic lifestyle, scurrying between here and London. Of course, she ended up losing the baby.'

'I'm sorry.'

'Really?' He stood up, walked across to the bar, poured himself another drink, and realised that he really was itching now to engage in an argument. Not that the cool, calm woman on the sofa had done anything to provoke one. Apart, he thought, from fuelling a raging resentment for having persuaded him, somehow, to share a part of himself that he had become quite accustomed to keeping locked away behind closed doors.

He sat down again, but before he could think of something suitably provocative to say she continued quietly, 'And what now? Does the stud farm take up all of your time?'

'Is this your bedside manner in operation?' he grated. 'Listen to the patient, deal with his rantings and ravings, but on no account encourage them?'

'You don't have to talk about this if you don't want to.'

'Why on earth should I care one way or the other? Divorce these days is hardly something to be kept under wraps, like a shameful secret. Is it?' She was so perfectly still. Like a living, breathing statue. 'I run a merchant bank in the city centre, partly from here, partly from my office in Dublin. And there are also a couple of companies in London. Investments, so to speak. You never know when a rainy day is going to arrive.'

'I guess not.'

She lowered her eyes and he wondered what she was thinking. He was surprised that her father hadn't mentioned it at some point, but then from what he had seen father and daughter didn't seem to enjoy a comfortable relationship. For the first time he felt a certain amount of sympathy for her. No wonder she had avoided visiting the family nest if the family in question was as distant as a stranger.

'Any more questions?' he asked, continuing to stare at her over the rim of his glass, and she raised her eyes to his.

'What was it that you wanted to discuss with me?'

'Ah, yes.' Now to the nitty-gritty. He carefully put down his glass, then folded his arms and looked directly at her. 'Your father. He's improved vastly over the past couple of weeks, and it's conceivable that some time in the next few months he might be able to return to work, but strictly on a part-time basis. He might retain some of his older patients, but the greater workload of the surgery...' He allowed his voice to taper off and let the silence inform her more succinctly than words would have done.

'That'll hurt him,' she said quietly. 'The surgery has been his lifeline. That particular surgery, he's been there...for ever! How does he feel about what you've just told me? About retiring?'

'He hasn't mentioned it to you himself?'

'We haven't had a great deal of time together,' Ellie said vaguely, re-crossing her legs.

'I think,' he said, when it became clear that she wasn't

going to enlarge on the subject, 'that he could accommodate the idea, under certain circumstances.'

'I don't suppose he will have a great deal of choice. Who have you got running the practice while he's been ill?'

'Young chap. Dr Selvern. You probably won't have heard of him. He's not a local man and I gather he's none too popular with the regulars.'

'How on earth do you find out these details?' Ellie asked, and he smiled at her, enjoying the amused surprise on her face. Of course, he thought, she wasn't sexy, not in the sense of a cleavage and legs to her armpits, but when she wasn't busy being guarded, like now, she really was rather...engaging.

'It's a small place, in case you'd forgotten. News here has a habit of spreading like wildfire. Selvern applied for the job of locum, assuming that it would eventually lead to a permanent placing, given the circumstances, but apparently he dislikes it around here. I met him, actually, a couple of weeks ago and he confessed that his ambition is to go abroad, to a Third World country. He's young and fired with ideals of saving the human race from itself.'

'And he prefers to do it on a grand scale?'

'It would seem so.'

'When does he intend to go?'

'As soon as possible. He's received confirmation of an appointment in Africa, a job which apparently he applied for some time ago, on the off chance. He didn't know that it would come through at all, never mind only weeks after accepting a post here.' He looked at her intently, wondering if she was beginning to get the general drift of his words, but her eyes remained clear and unblinking. Was the woman completely stupid? he thought with irritation.

'Well,' she said finally, 'I shall certainly keep my ear

to the ground, but, as you can imagine, being in London doesn't bring me into a great deal of contact with doctors who want to move to Ireland.'

'Mmm. Guess what we're looking for here is someone who's accustomed to living in the hicks.'

'Oh, I don't know, Dublin's not a million miles away.' She stood up, much to James's amazement. She didn't think that this was the end of the conversation, did she? For someone so intelligent, she certainly lacked perceptiveness when it came to reading between the lines.

'Where,' he asked, raising his eyebrows, 'are you going?'

'Bed, actually. It's been a long day.' She looked at him with some confusion, an expression which he decided he didn't much care for. Having wanted to see what lay beneath her cold, professional exterior, he now found those glimmers of femininity far too disconcerting. He reminded himself that his wife had also been one of those high-powered women, a temptation to any intelligent man. He had been a fool then, but he was smarter now. Now he knew that a woman like that was never worth the effort.

'We're not finished,' he said bluntly. 'Sit back down.'

'Please don't give me orders!'

There, that was better. Shutters up, defences at work. He could concentrate on what he was saying now, instead of being sabotaged by those damned emerald-green eyes and having to remind himself that types like her disagreed with his constitution.

'Then don't invite me to do so.' He watched with satisfaction as she sat back down, and ignored the 'let's just wind this up' expression on her face.

'Your father needs a replacement, Ellie. Someone he can trust, who is going to allow him the freedom of however much involvement he's capable of. As you yourself said, this surgery's his lifeline. How will he

survive if he's to be put out to pasture when his mind
is still so agile? How do you think he'll fill his time?
Knitting? A spot of embroidery?'

Ellie went bright red, but her voice didn't waver when
she spoke. He imagined that she would have liked to
throw something at him and he took a great deal of
pleasure in giving her a stare of infuriatingly sympathetic
understanding at the predicament he was obliged to present.

'In that case, he'll have to be fairly rigorous in the
interviews.'

'Why are interviews needed?'

'What do you mean?'

She leaned forward, and if it still hadn't sunk in, then
it was certainly beginning to. That much was evident in
the tenseness of her body and the suspicious narrowing
of her eyes.

'I propose that you return here to run the practice.'

There was the briefest of silences.

'Are you crazy?' You must be, her eyes told him. 'I
already have a job, a very exciting one, in London. How
can you even suggest that I return here to work?' Her
hands were gripping the sides of the chair.

'Why do you think that it's impossible to have a career outside of London?'

'I don't think that it's *impossible* to have a career
outside of London! I just think…'

'That you'd be stultified out here?'

'That's being overdramatic, but basically yes. If you
really want to know, I've worked very hard all my life
to get where I am now and I don't want to sit back and
spend the rest of my days behind a desk in a surgery
when I could be in a hospital, in the thick of things,
doing what I'm trained to do best.'

'There are some excellent hospitals in Dublin. You
could spend a certain amount of time in the surgery and

the rest in the hospital. Between your father and yourself, you could work it out.'

'Has my father asked you to put this...this proposition to me?'

'No, no, he hasn't.' James tried to control his temper. 'But he's worried about where he goes from here, worried about what's going to happen to the surgery if a suitable replacement isn't found.'

'You make it sound as though finding a suitable replacement is along the lines of looking for a needle in a haystack,' Ellie muttered. She stood up and headed towards the door, but before she could walk out James made sure that he was there, barring her way, his hand on the doorknob. If he could, he would have knocked some sense into her. It was certainly what he felt like doing right at that moment.

'And *you* make it sound as though your career is the only thing that matters in your life.' He spoke quietly, coldly.

'I've worked for it.'

'I don't deny that, but you can have a career here—and your father needs you.'

'He's never mentioned that to me.'

He could feel himself soften at the break in her voice.

'Maybe he doesn't know how to.' He gripped the doorknob hard. Next to him, she appeared so slight, like a piece of china. One move and she would break. He forced himself to think of the aggressive professional behind that frame. It stopped him from reaching out to touch her.

'I can help with the interviews,' she said quietly, looking down, so that her voice seemed to reach him from a distance.

'Apart from your job, what's keeping you in London? Is there a man there?' He realised, now that he had asked, that the question had been hovering on his lips for a while. He couldn't remember the last time any woman had aroused such intense curiosity in him.

'That's none of your business!' She looked up at him, blushing.

'It's no big secret if there is, is it?' I couldn't care less about her personal life, he told himself, but still he was reluctant to drop the topic, even though he could see that it embarrassed her.

'Well, if you must know, yes. I do happen to have a boyfriend.'

'What's he like?'

'Does it make a scrap of difference what Henry's like?'

'Henry? *Henry?*' He forced himself to sound amused. 'Is that his name?'

'Yes!'

'How much of a relationship can you two have, if you work all the hours under the sun?' He realised that he was being a bit like a dog with a bone and despised himself for it, but he couldn't seem to back off. The idea of Dr Eleanor Mills involved with a man was too intriguing to let go.

'We have a perfectly satisfactory relationship,' she retorted. 'Not that I have to explain any of this to you!'

The green eyes gleamed with emotion and he had the unnerving sensation of being exposed to fire, fascinated by its flames.

'''A perfectly satisfactory relationship''.' He leaned against the door so that any hope she might have had of flinging it open and walking out was now out of the question, and made a great show of giving the statement some thought. 'What an odd way to describe a seething romance. Wouldn't you agree?' When she didn't answer, he continued, in the same musing, speculative voice, 'Or perhaps it's not seething. Maybe it's more of a comfortable affair, like slipping into a pair of well-worn shoes. Is Henry a doctor as well?'

'Would you mind removing yourself from the door? I'd like to leave now.'

'Is he?'

'As a matter of fact, he is.'

'So you really can't see *that* much of one another. In which case, I would hardly categorise it as the sort of gripping romance that's going to keep you rooted to the city.'

'I don't much care what you'd categorise it as…'

'He could always move here with you, of course…'

'No, he could not!'

They stared at one another and for the first time in living memory James had the uncomfortable feeling of being utterly lost for words. What could he say to that? He would have liked to continue with his probing, but he knew that he was beginning to run the risk of sounding suspiciously over-curious. More to the point, he had no idea *why* he couldn't just let it go. Did it matter one way or the other what this mythical boyfriend was like?

He gave her an angry, frustrated look, half blaming her for arousing his curiosity in the first place, then smiled tightly at her.

'Think about your father.'

'Okay.' Ellie sighed, with a certain amount of defeat. 'I'll see what I can do about staying on here for a short while. But I insist on interviewing prospective candidates and I'll make sure that Father agrees with whatever choice is made.'

'Fine.' He removed himself from the door and stood aside. 'Now tell me, don't you feel better for that simple act of unselfishness?' He certainly did, and he decided that it was merely the simple pleasure gained from persuading someone to do the right thing.

He watched her as she left, but his mind was preoccupied. He felt irritated and displeased with himself. Antonia had been able to arouse anger in him, but it had always been a different sort of anger. An anger directed against her, for her sheer inability to compromise, and an anger directed against himself for not having seen that trait earlier on in their relationship. But he had been able to deal with that emotion, had been able to put it in perspective.

Now he felt merely unsettled, and because he couldn't pinpoint the reason why he couldn't find a way of dealing with the feeling.

Apart from immersing himself in his work, which he dutifully managed to do the following day. Phone calls, the usual sending and receiving of faxes, a trip into Dublin to his office—despite it being the weekend—and arranging a meeting with his accountant, whose happiness levels seemed to depend heavily on how well the books were looking. A satisfactory day with an enjoyable conclusion in the form of dinner with Amanda, a particularly glamorous friend with curves in all the right places.

James made a huge effort to be charming and several times he reminded himself that this was just the sort of company he relished. Light, flirtatious, undemanding. There was nothing wrong with the fact that what Amanda lacked in terms of intellectual horsepower was more than compensated for by a stunning figure, auburn hair that was as reflective as a mirror and magnificent blue eyes that combined just the right amount of innocence and knowledge. He was almost tempted to try to re-ignite the sexual passion they had shared six months ago.

Yes, very satisfactory. He strode into the house later that evening, really rather pleased with himself, and encountered Ellie in the sitting room, half-asleep on the sofa.

Instantly the self-satisfaction began draining away. She must have heard him come in because she opened her eyes and said, sitting up and pulling herself together, 'Oh, it's you.'

'Sorry to disappoint you,' he said sarcastically, trying to recapture his pleased frame of mind by conjuring up Amanda's image, and failing. He tossed his jacket onto a chair and sat down opposite her. 'I do happen to live here. Bumping into me is going to be something of an occupational hazard while we're under the same roof.' How, he asked himself, did she manage to put him in such a foul temper after only a minute?

'Which is something I wanted to discuss...'

'Did you speak to your father?'

'Yes. I told him that I'll be staying on here for a short while to sort things out and find a replacement for Dr Selvern.'

'Good.' His voice was clipped. He wondered whether she had spoken to Henry as well, but refrained from asking.

'Which brings me to the subject of the house. There's absolutely no need to remain here. I'm very grateful to you for having accommodated my father, but since I shall be with him the sooner we get back to his house the better.'

James grunted something fairly indecipherable and Ellie frowned at him, straining to hear.

'What did you say?'

'If you're quite certain. I assure you it's no bother having you here...'

'I'm absolutely certain.' She sat back, and linked her fingers together, and surveyed him impassively.

That's it, he thought. Her attitude. That's what puts me in a foul mood.

Eleanor Mills didn't talk to *him*. He could have been anyone, or anything, for that matter. She was talking again and he made an effort to concentrate on what she was saying. Something about trips and how many she would have to make to transport whatever her father had brought over to the Manor.

'How much stuff has he got here with him?'

'Not much. Clothes. Books.' He wondered how he had ever, albeit fleetingly, considered her appealing. With her no-nonsense manner and that clever look in her eyes that implied, without saying it outright, that fools wouldn't be tolerated. Didn't she know that men *never* found that a sexy trait in a woman?

'Right. That shouldn't be too much of a problem.' Ellie frowned into the distance, thinking. 'I shall go across first thing in the morning to get the house aired...'

'I could always send Josie across to clean it up for you.'

'That won't be necessary, thanks all the same. I'm more than capable of cleaning the place myself.'

'Just a suggestion.' Another highly unsexy trait, he thought. Blunt refusals of assistance. She probably scowled if some hapless man ever dared risk paying her a compliment. 'I merely thought,' he couldn't resist adding, 'that you might not be too enthusiastic about domestic chores. I know that high-powered women tend to consider these things beneath them.'

Ellie looked at him and refrained from rising to the bait. Instead, she stood up, yawned and asked a few polite questions about his day.

'Not going to bed already?' he said, watching her, noticing the way some of her hair had escaped from its bun and hung around her face in wispy strands. 'I do hope my company hasn't driven you out.'

'Not at all,' she answered pleasantly enough, looking at her watch. 'It's after ten, though, and I'm exhausted. I've had quite a day, what with one thing and another.' She glanced at him and he could see her controlling another yawn, which only served to irritate him further. Was he *that* big a bore? 'Nothing to do with your company.'

'Good, good!' he said in a hearty voice, stretching out his legs and continuing to look at her lazily. 'In that case, I assume you'll have no objection to joining me for dinner tomorrow night.'

'What?' She looked at him, open-mouthed. 'Why?'

Frankly, he couldn't remember ever having received such a lukewarm response to a dinner invitation in his entire life.

'To celebrate our new resident physician,' he said in the same hearty voice, which he hoped would disguise the fact that he was already regretting the invitation. We may not rub along, he wanted that tone to imply, but hey, I'm big enough to rise above that.

'Oh.' She thought for a while. 'Okay. Why not?'

'I'll pick you up at seven-thirty from your father's house.' What came over me? he thought. Temporary insanity? Oncoming illness? Brain shutdown?

'All right.' She hovered for a little longer—waiting, he thought sourly, like someone asking permission to be dismissed. Then she quietly left the room, shutting the door firmly behind her.

That, he thought, suddenly needing something to drink, is absolutely the last time I play the Samaritan. He poured himself a very weak whisky and soda, glared at the glass in his hand, and decided that he had every right to feel self-righteous over doing a good deed for someone incapable of appreciating it.

He decided that he felt well and truly sorry for that boyfriend of hers. Poor brute. Probably quite a nice chap, if misguided.

Only much later, in bed, did he realise that he had been so busy grumbling to himself that he had completely forgotten to drink the whisky and soda.

CHAPTER THREE

ELLIE had only brought one dress with her. A plain pale blue dress, simply cut and packed primarily because of its amazing ability to withstand creasing, however small it was folded. She had not anticipated going anywhere in the few days she had expected to be here. Consequently the dress, worn with her one other pair of shoes—some tan sandals—still made her look as though she was off to do some shopping, rather than to have dinner in a restaurant with a man to whom she increasingly felt she had to prove something. What, exactly, she had no idea.

Only her hair and an application of make-up made a difference to her appearance. For the first time since she had arrived, she decided to wear her hair loose. She washed it, dried it and brushed it, then scrutinised the effect in the mirror. Long, fair hair, curling a bit at the bottom. Hair that gleefully rebutted the serious, intelligent face. Hair, she had always thought, that was ideally suited to a woman who laughed a lot, flirted heavily and generally flung herself around. Not the hair of a hardworking paediatric doctor. She should have had it cut years ago. Keeping it long had been her one small rebellion.

Then she carefully applied some make-up: lipstick, blusher and mascara.

The dress, she decided, finally stepping back from the mirror, didn't look quite so drab now.

Her father, when she went downstairs, made no comment. It crossed Ellie's mind that that could well be his entire view of her. No comment. How, she wondered despairingly, was she going to cope?

'I shouldn't be long, Father,' she told him, artistically arranging some home-made quiche and salad on a plate, feeling him follow her efforts with a marked lack of enthusiasm. He had once told her—when she was no more than fourteen, and after she had spent hours elaborately preparing a meal for him—that her mother had been a superb cook. Then he had looked at her food with the same look that he produced every time she cooked anything for him—a look that made comparisons, and found her wanting. Her father had always been so good at that, at implying his disappointment rather than just expressing it outright. How could she ever fight the thoughts that he kept inside his head?

'Don't hurry back on account of me. I'm not completely incapacitated.'

'I'll get James to leave the telephone number of the restaurant before we go. Just in case.'

'Just in case what?' he asked in an argumentative voice. 'In a minute you'll be suggesting a babysitter.' He stared at the quiche as though expecting it to rise up from the plate and attack him, then began eating, carefully wiping his mouth between bites.

'There's pudding in the fridge,' Ellie told him. 'I made some fresh fruit salad.'

'Invalid food.'

It was the normal run of conversation between them, but she was too busy feeling nervous to pay it as much attention as she normally would have.

'It's healthy food, Father.'

'Any food that can be eaten without the use of teeth is invalid food,' he informed her. Her father, she had long ago realised, was fond of making provocative remarks to her—angling, she suspected, for what she would call a pointless argument and what he would no doubt call a healthy debate. Right now, Ellie felt like indulging in neither.

'A hearty fry-up won't do you any good!' she said, losing patience. 'You know that as well as I do!'

'No need to fly off the handle over a simple observation,' he muttered testily. 'Women!'

On any other occasion, she knew that she would never have snapped at her father. She would have tiptoed around him, trying to placate and ease the onset of troubled waters. Now, though, things were different. She wasn't here for a fleeting visit and she didn't know whether she could cope with an indefinite period of enforced politeness.

'No need to argue over every point,' she said, with equal testiness. 'Men!' They stared at one another and she felt that horrid, churning feeling of being a child again, about to be reprimanded for some very understandable show of infantile temper. 'I'm sorry, Father, I didn't mean to snap.'

'The quiche is very nice,' he responded stiffly.

Into the silence, the doorbell rang, and she flew to the door with a feeling of relief. What on earth was wrong with her, reacting like that?

'Good Lord,' James said with exaggerated amazement. 'You're ready. Most women usually make a point of being slightly late. You must be the exception that proves the rule. Where's your father?'

'In the kitchen,' Ellie replied, following him through.

She waited by the door while the two men chatted for five minutes, and as soon as they were in the car she said brusquely, 'I'd rather not be too late tonight. It's Father's first night back at home and he might be a little nervous about being on his own.' She kept her eyes firmly fixed ahead of her, but was aware of him inclining his head slightly, throwing her a sidelong glance.

'He didn't seem particularly nervous to me. How did the move go?'

'Fine, thank you.' For some reason she felt angry with him, and a bit of a fool for having taken such pains to look attractive when she might just as well have spared herself the effort. She would have felt far more at home with her hair tidied away and her face bare of make-up. 'We only needed to do one trip, as it turned out.'

'And you went into the surgery?'

'Dr Selvern was very helpful.'

'He would be,' James agreed with a dry laugh. 'He sees you as his rescuer. I bet he couldn't wait to throw those patient files at you. Has he given you an exact date for departure?'

'Friday,' Ellie said.

'Short notice.'

'Well, there's not much point in him hanging around, is there?' she snapped. 'I might just as well take over and then I can set the interview procedures in motion.' She knew that her behaviour was bordering on rude, but the little, inconsequential flare-up with her father had left her nerves feeling frayed, and now, here in the car with James, she could feel her frayed nerves beginning to shred quite badly at the seams.

'Can't wait to get back to the busy London life, can you?'

'It's what I'm used to.'

'How do you know that you wouldn't like something more peaceful if you've never tried it?' James asked curiously.

'I'm not a peaceful person!' Ellie snapped, saying the first thing that came into her head and regretting it the minute the words were out.

'What does that mean?' He shot her another quick but comprehensive look, eyebrows raised.

'I guess it means that I thrive on a certain amount of

pressure.' Did it? Was that what she meant? He seemed
to have a talent for knocking through her well-mannered,
controlled façade and exposing all sorts of untidy things
underneath.

'You'll have high blood pressure by the time you're
forty,' he responded agreeably.

'Thank you for your medical opinion. The same might
well be said of you—or do men handle stress without
that irritating little side-effect of high blood pressure?'
She shouldn't have accepted this wretched invitation,
she thought. She hadn't been thinking straight at the
time.

'You are an extremely argumentative woman,' he said
conversationally, and unfortunately there was no time to
rise to that particular bait because they had arrived at
the restaurant—a small, expensive-looking place cosily
tucked away between two offices.

Inside it had all the charm of a place that prided itself
on its good food, good ambience, and a well-to-do cli-
entele. They were personally greeted by the owner, who
exchanged sufficient jolly remarks with James to make
Ellie realise that he was a familiar face here, and they
were shown to a table in the corner.

'I'd recommend the fish,' he said as she waded her
way through a menu roughly the size of the table. Everything was in French, without benefit of translations, and
she readily agreed to his suggestion. French was a language she knew only in passing and, left to her own
devices, she was quite sure that she would end up with
a plateful of something she didn't like.

He appeared to have completely forgotten their little
war of words of a few moments before. Wasn't that just
typical of a man like James Kellern? she thought, still
simmering. Fond of making provocative, sweeping gen-
eralisations and then, frustratingly, not seeing his own
arguments through to the end. Dear Henry, she thought

suddenly, never argued. Thank heavens. Perhaps she had been taking him for granted lately.

Years ago, when she had first met Henry, she had still been smarting from her ill-fated relationship with Cameron Clark. Henry, in comparison, had seemed like a long drink of water after a particularly gruelling hike through a desert. But that was a long time ago and Cameron was no longer in her head. Now, though, she could appreciate Henry's good points—James Kellern, with his arrogance, his amused speculation on areas of her life that didn't concern him, and his damned self-assurance, was making sure of that.

'So,' he said, once their drinks had been brought, 'what else do you need to do before you establish yourself here?'

Ellie frowned at his choice of words, but decided not to comment. 'I shall have to go to London at some point, probably in the next few days,' she answered, thinking aloud. 'Pay a visit to the hospital, tie up any loose ends there. Also, pack some clothes. I only brought enough to last a few days.'

'You don't need to worry about a wardrobe, though, do you? Don't doctors just fling white coats over everything?'

'Yes,' she said a little starchily. 'We do wear white coats. That doesn't mean that we wear any old rubbish underneath them just because the patients won't notice one way or the other.'

'Why not?'

A waiter brought them their starters—small, artistically displayed salads on very small, gold-rimmed plates.

'Because,' she said patiently, 'I happen to take some pride in how I look.'

'Which is how?'

'How what?' she asked, puzzled. She dug into the

salad with some regret, hating to disturb the professional beauty of the arrangement.

'How do you like to look?' He glanced across the table and his grey eyes held hers for a fraction of a moment before she looked away and continued eating.

'I like looking smart,' she told him in a brisk voice.

'How does Henry like you to look?'

'Please leave Henry out of the conversation!'

'Why should I? I thought that women liked talking about their loved ones.' His face was serious but she suspected, grimly, that he was laughing at her. Again. No doubt adding the description 'smart' to all the other ones stored in his head. *A smartly turned out woman, usually to be found striding manfully around the hospital wards in a white coat. Crisp, no-nonsense manner. Love life with all the magic of a leftover dinner.*

There was another reason why she didn't particularly want to get him onto the subject of Henry. She still hadn't told him of her decision to move back to Ireland, albeit not permanently. She had decided to break the news face to face when she was next in London.

'How did your father react when you told him you had decided to stay?'

'As expected,' she said, sighing. 'He refused to entertain the idea.'

'Was that what you expected?' James looked surprised, but then how was he to know the sort of relationship she had with her father? 'I would have thought he would be rather pleased.'

'Father hates the thought of accepting help.' Especially when it comes from me, she thought. 'He blustered and protested and waved aside every reason I could come up with until I eventually just told him outright that he was wasting his time, that I was going to stay until something permanent was sorted out whether he liked it or not.'

It had, she could have added, been another battle along the lines of all the battles they had fought since time immemorial. No shouting, no raised voices, but still the same pride and stubbornness that made every suggestion fraught with the possibility of rejection.

'He said I was a fool for even considering the move, that Dr Selvern was more than capable of finding a replacement.'

'Not what he's told me in the past.'

'Yes, well, you probably have a better relationship with my father than I have.' She hadn't meant to say that and she blushed hotly at the lapse. 'I mean...'

'I know what you mean. You might find that your enforced stay here does you both more good than either of you expect.'

'Maybe.' Ellie seriously doubted that, but she shrugged and allowed the matter to ride. Talking about her father always ended up making her feel like a colossal failure, despite all her outward trappings of success, and she changed the subject without even thinking about it. She was so accustomed to veering away from subjects too close to home that she hardly noticed the shift in conversation.

'When,' he asked, after they had exhausted polite conversation, 'are you planning on going to London?'

Ellie shrugged. Several glasses of wine with their excellent fish had lowered her levels of defensiveness. She had even caught herself laughing at some of the things he had said.

'Some time this week, I guess,' she answered. 'I want to get Father's house sorted out first.'

'I wouldn't have thought it would be too messy,' James said, surprised.

'It isn't.' She frowned. 'It just needs some redecoration here and there.' She had forgotten how run-down it had become over the years. She was quite sure that the wallpaper in some of the rooms had not been changed since she was a child, and the house had a general air of somewhere lived in by a man who really didn't care much what the place looked like, just so long as it was clean. If she was going to stay there, even for a short while, she would do her best to make sure that she pulled her weight. Anyway, having something to do would keep her busy, cover over all those cracks in their relationship which silence and inaction intensified.

'And you plan on having that done by the end of the week? Sounds ambitious.'

'Are you being sarcastic?' It hardly mattered, since she was beginning to feel too pleasantly mellow to do anything energetic like take offence. 'I shall go into Dublin tomorrow and choose some wallpaper, and then I shall do what I can and take it from there. If needs be, I'll arrange for a decorator to come in and finish it off.'

'I guess a busy woman like you just doesn't have the time to do such things herself.'

'I have no intention of picking an argument with you, James,' Ellie commented sweetly. 'Anyway, you're absolutely right. A busy woman like myself just doesn't have the time.' She finished off her wine and regarded the empty glass with surprise. 'Not,' she continued, 'that I wouldn't like to do it all myself. I would. It's just difficult fitting things in.'

He gave her a long, serious look, as though he was about to add something to that remark.

'I shall be going to London on Thursday,' he said, after a while. 'We can travel over together in my private plane.'

'No, thanks; really, there's no need.' In a muddled way, she knew that she didn't want to be cooped up anywhere with James Kellern. A couple of hours over dinner, with plenty of people around, was all right. A couple of hours in the air, however, with no one around at all and without even the distraction of a meal, was not worth considering.

'Why not?' he asked bluntly. He sat back in his chair, beckoned the waiter across for coffee without taking his eyes off her face, and then folded his arms.

His body language, she thought, could be very off-putting. If he had leaned over in a chummy, confidential manner, then she was sure she could have laughingly come up with some excuse. As it was, she felt pinned to the spot and devoid of excuses.

'Well?' he persisted. 'You're not afraid of me, are you?'

'Of course I'm not! Why on earth should I be?' She tried to inject the right balance of amusement and incredulity into her voice, but realised that she had sounded vaguely anxious and not at all incredulous.

'Because I'm a man?'

'Don't be absurd. I'm not totally inexperienced.' But she was feeling less and less in control by the minute, and she took refuge in her coffee cup.

'Perhaps on a professional level, but I get the feeling that on a personal level you're quite adept at keeping your distance.'

'I happen to be involved with a man!'

He appeared not to have heard that. 'It would save you a great deal of inconvenience,' he pointed out smoothly. 'And,' he carried on, when she didn't answer, 'you needn't have anything to fear from me.'

'I told you, I am not afraid of you. Grateful to you, yes, for making sure that my father was looked after when he came out of hospital, and obviously, as your neighbour, I hope that we can have an amicable relationship, but fear doesn't enter into the equation. Fear of what?'

'Fear of me making a pass at you? I get the feeling

that you see me as a threat and you respond accordingly.'

There was a short silence between them, but it felt very long indeed. The sounds in the restaurant seemed to have intensified, and she could feel her skin breaking out into a shimmer of perspiration. If only she could get her mouth into working order, she would inform him, as coldly as she could, that he must have an ego the size of a battleship to think that he had that sort of effect on her.

'You're not my type, you know,' he said conversationally. 'I was married to a career woman like yourself. I have firsthand experience of the type.'

'The type?' Ellie looked at him in disbelief. 'You make it sound as though all women who hold down a job are despicable. This is the twentieth century, just in case you hadn't realised!'

'I'm not talking about women who hold down jobs,' James said evenly. 'I'm talking about women with careers. The two are poles apart.'

'There's nothing wrong with a woman wanting to achieve something in her life.'

'Absolutely not.'

'Anyway,' she heard herself say defensively, 'has it occurred to you that you're no more my type than I am yours?' A cool, controlled laugh after this little statement would have been enough, but Ellie felt neither cool nor controlled. 'I've had firsthand experience of a man like you, and it left a lot to be desired.'

'Really?' He sat forward slightly, and she could have kicked herself for the slip-up.

'Delicious meal.' She shot him a steely look and he smiled slowly.

'Relax,' he said easily. 'I'm not about to quiz you on your past. I don't really care what you did or didn't do or, for that matter, what you're doing or not doing now.

But I do care about your father and I fully intend to make sure that you do your duty and wait until he's capable of coping, before you fly back to London and the boyfriend and the high-powered job.'

'You must be crazy if you think that you can tell me what to do!'

He smiled at her, but there was no humour behind the smile, just a certain amount of determination that alternately chilled and angered her.

'Try me.'

'I'll stay until a replacement is found, but if needs be I shall choose the replacement on my own, if Father proves uncooperative. I have a life to get back to!'

'Correction: you see your father as a chore. I can't help how you feel about him, but I won't let you scarper off back to London until you've seen things through down here.'

'*You* won't *let* me? Just who do you think you are?'

'Someone who knows the meaning of compassion.'

Ellie felt her skin begin to burn. She hadn't raised her voice, not by a fraction, and she wouldn't, because she wasn't a shouting kind of person, but, dammit, she felt like yelling her head off. How *dared* he?

'And you imagine that, as a doctor, *I* have no compassion? Is that what you think?'

'I think that compassion, like charity, starts at home.' They stared at one another and she was overwhelmed by the utter pointlessness of continuing the argument. James Kellern was a law unto himself and trying to convince him otherwise was hardly worth the effort. She lowered her eyes and clasped her hands tightly together on her lap. Let him think he'd won this round, by all means. She would do her best here, she would find her replacement, but if he seriously considered that she would somehow end up staying on here permanently, then he was shouting uselessly into the wind. He would discover that in due course.

'This is ridiculous.' She attempted a smile, or something, at least, that wasn't a scowl. 'I assure you that I have Father's welfare at heart.'

'Fine. Now, I shall be leaving quite early on Thursday morning. Around seven. Do you want me to call for you or not?'

'Yes, all right,' Ellie said in a forced voice. 'If you're quite sure. I'll be ready.'

'I won't be coming back till Friday, though. You can either make your own way back or you can arrange for the nurse to stay the night with your father.'

'I'll make my own way back,' she said quickly. She stood up to go to the Ladies, somewhat alarmed to find that her feet didn't appear as steady as they usually did. In fact, none of her felt quite as steady as normal.

It wouldn't do, she thought as she peered into the mirror and re-applied some of her lipstick. She was a professional, and if she was going to be working here for the next month or so she had to slap down these strange responses to him. She had to stop letting him get under her skin.

But he confused her. She wasn't accustomed to having strange responses to anything. Her life had always been focused, ordered. It had had to be that way. Her father had always been a taciturn, authoritarian figure. A strong, guiding hand, but one not given to emotional outbursts, nor to indulging them in her. She'd been sent to boarding-school at the age of seven. She had learned, from early on, to be independent, to achieve, because, without having to be told, she had groped her way into an understanding that achievement was the only thing that her father expected of her.

So why did James Kellern and his opinions of her make her head spin like this? Why did she find it so hard to distance herself from him, as she did with every other man? Was it because she was back on home ground and at odds with herself?

She could not come up with any other reason, apart from the possibility that perhaps their personalities just didn't click, and because he was so damned forthright he didn't bother to use courtesy to camouflage their mutual antagonism.

It was the only thing that made any sense and it would have to do. She was a sensible person and right now she needed to instil reason and logic into reactions that were unreasonable and illogical.

She stood back from her reflection, feeling better now that she had successfully analysed the situation, and left the cloakroom decidedly more in control.

She had expected him to be waiting for her, perhaps by the door, or at least standing by the table in readiness to leave, but he wasn't. He was still sitting down, and, more to the point, her chair was occupied.

Ellie stopped in her tracks and, unobserved, looked at the woman sitting opposite him. Straight, copper-coloured hair to her shoulders, widely spaced eyes, wide, voluptuous mouth. And, judging from what she could see of the rest of her, a body to match the face. They were laughing, and the woman was leaning forward towards him, elbows on the table, emerald-green dress revealing enough cleavage, Ellie thought, to grip a pencil.

She walked briskly towards them and when she was at the table the flame-haired woman glanced at her, laughing, and apologised for sitting in her chair.

'But I spotted Angel from across the restaurant and I couldn't stop myself from coming over to say hello!'

'Angel?' Ellie looked at James with raised eyebrows.

'My little nickname for James, when we were going out together.'

'Oh, right. Very sweet.' Yuk.

'Ellie, this is Amanda Evans. Mandy, this is Eleanor Mills. She's here to take over from George, running the surgery.'

'I was very sorry to hear about your dad,' Amanda said, standing up and thrusting out one elegant hand for Ellie to shake. The emerald-green dress, which comprised very little up top, was similarly lacking in fabric at the bottom. It fitted the tall, curvy body like cling film to mid-thigh.

'Thank you.' Ellie shook hands perfunctorily.

'Have your seat back. I've got to go anyway. My sister's been champing at the bit to leave for the past fifteen minutes.' Another dazzling smile. 'We're off to see what the nightlife has to offer. Why don't you two join us?'

'Feel free, James,' Ellie said. 'The only nightlife I'm heading for at the moment involves my bed.'

'Lucky girl,' Amanda said with a throaty laugh, looking at both of them. 'I'm sure Angel will take good care of you.' She strolled off in the manner of someone who knew that all eyes were focused on her, and Ellie glanced at James, stony-faced.

'You might have set her straight on our relationship,' she said stiffly.

'What for? Does it bother you what a perfect stranger thinks of you?'

'No, but if I have to have a reputation I prefer to earn it rather than have it thrust upon me.'

'Your reputation hardly matters, though, does it, considering the short length of time you're going to be around?'

He was grinning at her, as relaxed and amused at her discomfiture as she had ever seen him.

'Anyway,' he said, standing up, 'you look as though you're ready to leave.'

'There really is no need to drop me back,' Ellie said awkwardly as they walked towards the door. 'Please don't feel that you have to drive me home. I'm more than capable of finding my own way back.'

'No trouble. I'm a little too old for nightclubs anyway.'

'But not too old for the girls who go there, so I see.' For a moment there, standing next to that fresh-faced, stunningly beautiful woman, she had felt like an ageing matron, someone whose youth had flown away without her even realising it. She had a vivid picture of herself in ten years' time, forty-four years old, hurrying from ward to ward whilst ever younger interns trailed respectfully behind her taking notes. No children, no family to return to. Probably no Henry either. It wasn't a very joyful picture.

'Oh, I'm no cradle-snatcher,' he said lazily as they went outside and headed for the car, which was parked across the road. 'Mandy's twenty-five years old. A big girl.'

'Big enough to take care of herself when you inevitably decide that she's outstayed her welcome?'

He opened the passenger door for her, and once they were inside the car he turned to her and asked, 'Did she strike you as a bitter woman?'

'No, but...'

'But nothing. Your life is so compartmentalised that you can't conceive of a relationship that isn't necessarily destined for the altar.'

'That's not true!'

He started the car, driving slowly and smoothly through Dublin.

'Isn't it? I bet you've never done anything rash, anything utterly spontaneous, in your life!'

'We're not talking about me.'

'Well, have you? Was this mystery man you mentioned earlier on your little flirtation with reckless behaviour?'

'That's none of your business and I wouldn't call jumping into bed with all and sundry utterly spontaneous.'

He laughed, but there was a hard edge to his laughter. 'You make me sound as though I'm some kind of sex maniac! Mandy and I liked one another, we enjoyed each other's company, and, yes, we went to bed together.'

'And this coming from the man who said that he had no time for the female sex.'

'Perhaps I phrased that wrongly,' James said, changing gear to overtake a car and leaving his hand on the gear-shaft. 'Perhaps I should have said that I have no time for commitment to a woman.'

'And the women you go out with unanimously agree with that?'

'I wouldn't go out with them otherwise.' He shrugged. 'I made the mistake of marriage once. I don't intend to make it again.'

'And what does Amanda do for a living?' Ellie asked politely. 'Does she conform to your ideal woman who spends all her free time grooming herself for the big moment when you, or whoever else, arrives to take her out?'

'You didn't care for me classifying you as a career woman, did you?' he asked curiously.

'I don't care for anyone classifying me.'

'Mandy works. She's a fitness instructor at a gym.'

'Very cerebral,' Ellie muttered, hotly aware of jealousy running through her veins like lava. What would it be like to have all that social *savoir faire* at your fingertips? To be outrageous, safe in the knowledge that the whole world would smile in response? Never to fight a battle in a man's world with only your intelligence as ammunition? To be able, she thought with shame, to attract a man like James Kellern, the sort of man who

enjoyed women, women who were obviously female—
not women like her, who had grown accustomed to con-
cealing their femininity until it was too late to resurrect
it.

'Now who's classifying who?' he asked, breaking into
her thoughts. 'Do you consider yourself a better human
being than Amanda merely because you have a degree
in medicine and an important job at a teaching hospital
in London?'

'I don't want to pursue this conversation.' She stared
out of the window, her body tense.

'Why not? Because it makes you feel uncomfortable
to talk about anything that's not absolutely impersonal?'

Ellie bit her lip and continued staring. She tried hard
not to blink because she had a feeling that if she blinked
she would start to cry. Not because she was angry or
upset with him, but because he somehow made her feel
sorry for herself.

And being back here in Ireland didn't help either. In
London, she was surrounded by the sheer density of
buildings and people, propelled along a certain path,
without room to pay much attention to anything that
wasn't involved with work.

Here, there was space to listen to the sound of herself
and to the sounds of dreams and hopes that lay just outside her consciousness—dreams and hopes of yesterday
that would never be realised now.

'Are you planning to let your father help you at all in
the surgery?' James asked from beside her, and she wondered whether he had caught whatever vibes had been
emanating from her. Maybe he had had his little laugh
at her expense and was ready to move on. She was grateful for the change in conversation.

They were out of Dublin and very nearly back at the
house. Just enough time for her to manufacture some
semblance of brightness.

When the car stopped, she undid her seatbelt, opened the car door and started to thank him politely for taking her out to dinner.

'I'll walk you to the door,' he said, 'so you can save the pretty speeches for there.'

He followed her up the path to the front door, where she proceeded to fumble inside her bag for her keys, very much aware of him standing next to her, with his hands in his pockets.

'Well, thank you once again. And I'll be ready on Thursday. Thank you for the offer. It really will save me a great deal of time.' She paused, at a loss for anything further to say, and looked up at him. The cool air and the drive back had cleared her head, but now the stillness and the darkness conspired to bring back that muddled feeling again, and she found that she couldn't look away from his face.

'So are you glad that you accepted my dinner invitation? Despite the fact that it's such a mammoth effort fighting down your disapproval of me?' He sounded as though he really didn't care one way or the other what her opinion of him was. If anything, he found her disapproval amusing.

'The meal was delicious,' Ellie told him, dragging her gaze away from him. She could feel his sheer masculine energy close to her. It made the hairs on her arms stand on end. How was this possible when she disliked him so intensely? 'Thank you. Well, goodnight, then.'

He didn't answer. Or rather he did, but soundlessly. He just lifted her chin so that she was looking at him once again, and as his head drew closer down her lips parted, partly in protest, partly in anticipation.

Had this been on her mind ever since she had first laid eyes on him? She couldn't believe it, but then her body was telling another story as it curved against his and their tongues met. She felt her breasts ache under her dress and had a yearning sensation like nothing she had ever had before. As though she would melt at any moment. A dangerous sensation. The sheer, wild loss of self-control that it induced made her pull away from him and she found that she was shaking.

'Is that your usual way of saying goodnight?' she asked, torn between a display of outrage and an attempt at sophisticated banter. She opted for the latter.

'No, not usually,' James said. 'Usually I get inside the house as well.'

'I see. Well, it's safe for you to assume that that won't be the case this time round.'

She sounded prim and proper and she thought of Amanda, with her inviting come-hither laughter and that short, revealing dress, and wondered bleakly whether there really wasn't something missing from her life. Something vital.

'See you on Thursday.' He gave her a brief nod, and she waited by the front door, watching him as he strolled down the path, got into his car and headed off.

Her father was obviously asleep, as the house was completely dark, and she didn't want to switch any lights on. In the darkness, she could pretend that she was invisible, and that a kiss, which had lasted less than two minutes, hadn't sent her senses reeling.

She made a very big effort to imagine herself as Dr Eleanor Mills, one of the bright sparks in the field of paediatric medicine. Eleanor Mills striding through the hospital, treating her patients, hair neatly tied back, clad in a sober-coloured suit with her white coat over it. Eleanor Mills, in a dress of similarly sober colour, having dinner with Henry, a comfortable, unthreatening dinner where no arguments reared their heads to disturb the placid surface of their relationship.

Had James Kellern been kissing *her*? she wondered. A woman with feelings, emotions, insecurities which she had never even known she possessed? Or had he simply been satiating his curiosity? Kissing the paediatric doctor simply to gauge whether she was capable of a response?

The latter, she suspected.

Questions like this…responses as wild as a raging river trying to barge its way through a wall… She would be glad to get back to London, even if it was only for one day. She needed to. She needed to re-slot herself back into the role she had played all her life. She could feel danger edging towards her, yet when she turned around to confront it there was nothing there. The danger was inside her.

London and Henry—that was just what she needed. Desperately.

CHAPTER FOUR

OF COURSE, James knew that it had been a mistake to offer to take Ellie with him to London on his private jet. What had begun as a grim determination to get Eleanor Mills out of London and where she belonged—here, at least temporarily, by her father's side—seemed to have turned into a mild attack of curiosity, a wanting to find out about this composed, efficient young woman who had once been his neighbour.

Now, he was as grimly determined as ever. Frankly, he had seen nothing to make him change his opinion of her, so how was it that the curiosity was threatening to overtake him completely?

He drove back to his house, hugely irritated to find that he couldn't stop thinking about the damned woman.

The worst of it was that he really couldn't understand why she was on his mind at all. He hadn't been lying when he had told her that he was simply not attracted to women like her. He had had his fingers burnt once with his ex-wife and since then he had always made sure that he steered far away from pushy career women. That wasn't to say that he confined himself to airheads, but, he had to admit now, his recent girlfriends, enjoyable though they were, would never qualify as rocket scientists.

The house was in darkness when he arrived back, and he made his way up the stairs without bothering to switch on any lights. If he was destined to be plagued by uninvited musings on Eleanor Mills then he might as well give in and get them out of the way before he fell asleep.

It was his experience that women did not occupy a vast amount of his thoughts. They fell, in fact, quite a long way behind work. Not as intellectually invigorating as his business concerns, but pleasurable enough. It was baffling that he should be devoting any of his time at all to thinking about Eleanor Mills, since, he reflected, it was hardly as though her company was the height of relaxation. His usual line in banter tended to desert him the minute she appeared, and even when he managed to resurrect some of it his attempts to be charming were met with stony silence.

He undressed while still on the move, a habit which his ex-wife had deplored, and one which he had indulged in the minute she had disappeared from the scene.

He stripped off his shirt, followed by his trousers, and after he had washed his face slipped between the covers with only his boxer shorts on.

He had intended to do some work before retiring to bed. There were some faxes that had to be dealt with and a list of accounts which Frank, his estate manager, had left on his desk for him to look at, but there was no chance that any of it would be done, and there was even less point in trying. He wouldn't be able to concentrate, at least not until his head was cleared of Eleanor Mills.

He lay flat on the bed with his hands behind his head and stared up at the ceiling. Maybe if he thought about his ex-wife he would be able to draw a few useful comparisons between her and Eleanor, and get rid of his unwanted thoughts.

Just thinking of Antonia was enough to throw him into a foul frame of mind. He found it hard to remember what the good times with her had been like, even though he knew there must have been some or else marriage would never have featured on the agenda. The problem was that the bad times had always been far more frequent. And a lot of them had stemmed from the fact that Antonia had been wedded to her career, without, it had transpired over time, the benefit of that switch-off device that most people had—the device that allowed them to leave work behind when they stepped through the front door.

'And you, Eleanor Mills,' he said aloud to the ceiling, 'are precisely the same.' Worse, he thought, if anything. Doctors, especially those who specialised, were notorious for never being able to switch off.

She probably only had a tiny portion of her mind on what was happening outside work. The rest would be focused on patients. He imagined, with gusto, scenarios of her with Henry, both of them earnestly discussing illnesses, or whatever else doctors talked about in their spare time, both sleeping on separate sides of the same bed, with their beepers at the ready. He almost laughed aloud at the image.

When you got right down to it, he thought, she had probably forgotten the art of enjoying herself somewhere along the way. Enjoyment for enjoyment's sake. Basically, a boring person. Not lethal in the way Antonia had been, because medicine, at least, was a vocation that required compassion, but boring nevertheless.

Boring and, of course, selfish. He had found it amazing that old Dr Mills had been so reluctant to contact his only child after the stroke. He supposed, grudgingly, that there was a certain lack of warmth between them, but as far as he was concerned that in no way excused Ellie for her patent lack of filial duty over the past few years. He strenuously reminded himself that he had virtually had to hold a gun to her head to get her to stay, and even now that she had agreed she really couldn't wait to leave. Whatever form the outside package took, career women all fell into the same category: obsessed with their jobs.

And yet, over the next few days, wayward thoughts

kept jumping into his head at the least appropriate moments.

When his next-in-command made an inoffensive remark on Wednesday afternoon, after a particularly gruelling meeting with clients, along the lines of 'Are you all right, James? Seem a little distracted', James heard himself launch aggressively into hated self-defence. It wasn't like him. He had always been a firm believer in self-control—why shout when a low voice could achieve just as much?

'Just a little under the weather, Richard,' he mumbled by way of apology, wondering if perhaps he had inadvertently hit the nail on the head there. 'Must be coming down with something. A touch of flu, maybe.'

Richard looked at him with concern. 'Right. Thought it must be something like that. At one point, I even thought that you were losing interest in the deal.'

'Not a chance!' James said, with a lot of exaggerated *bonhomie*. They strolled out of the boardroom and he tried to remember what, precisely, the client had agreed to. He knew that he had won the battle, but he couldn't quite recall how. Must have been operating on autodrive.

'Well, that's a relief.' Richard smiled, and paused at the door to his office. 'Maybe you should take to bed for the next couple of days. See this infection off, whatever it is. Surely London can wait?'

London? Wait? He realised, with some chagrin, that he had been quietly looking forward to that wretched plane trip with that wretched woman, and the realisation threatened to send him hurtling once more into a bad mood. He forced himself to laugh off the suggestion.

'You worry too much, Richard,' he said heartily. 'Sign of old age, you know.' Richard was only four years older than him, but that small age gap had always been a predictable source of good-natured joking between the two men.

'Well, if you do go,' he replied, grinning, 'make sure that you take it easy. No wine, women and song.'

'I don't know,' James said, returning the smile, though with effort, and thinking of long, blonde hair and infuriatingly composed features. 'Wine, women and song are generally accepted as the best cure for on-coming infection.' Richard was happily married with four children, and made a great show of envying James's exploits with the opposite sex.

Later that night it occurred to James that there was quite a bit that he envied in his assistant. For a start, the stability of his marriage. He had always assumed that he had successfully washed his hands of an essentially weak institution. Now, though, he wondered what it must be like to be in a state of happily wedded bliss, immune to all those disturbing, niggling little feelings that were as-sailing him at the moment.

He really would have to get a grip on himself, he thought. Sixteen was an emotional age he had no desire to revisit. When he saw Ellie in the morning, he would make sure that his untrammelled curiosity was kept firmly in place. He would remind himself that she was, in fact, an open and closed book. Not to mention the little fact of her being involved with someone, anyway. Someone eminently suited to her, no doubt.

He permitted himself a rueful grin at his own stupid-ity. Perhaps his diet of women—the few there had been—had been too relentlessly similar over the past few years. Just maybe there was such a thing as a surfeit of glamour, which was probably why he was finding the intrusion of a woman so entirely different as intriguing as a scientist discovering a new species of microscopic life.

It was hardly as though she showed the slightest in-terest in him, anyway!

That little gem of a thought came to him out of the

blue the following morning, as he was dressing. He paused in fixing his tie and looked into the mirror. It was a testament to his own maturity, he decided, that he was not the slightest bit piqued by this. After all, you won a few, you lost a few—and it really didn't matter anyway, since in terms of winning she was not even on the list.

True, he had kissed her after that dinner. But briefly, almost as an afterthought. A goodnight kiss. He had a fleeting recollection of how his limbs had felt after that brush of lips, and hurriedly finished dressing.

She was dressed and waiting for him as soon as he arrived at the house, a little before seven. Her hair, he noticed immediately, was very severely pulled back from her face. Not an errant strand to be spotted. Her suit was exactly what he would have expected a doctor to wear. Grey, with a longish jacket and a skirt that was just the right length to avoid being either stylish or provocative. All that was missing was a pair of spectacles and a stethoscope around the neck, and—oh, yes—the obligatory white coat.

'Have you quite finished…?' Ellie asked politely.

It would be pointless trying to explain that his appraisal had been involuntary, so he glanced at his watch instead and then asked where her father was.

'Wouldn't mind saying hello before we leave. We've got a bit of time,' he said.

'He's in the kitchen trying to get enthused over an omelette.' She nodded in the direction of the kitchen and followed him, though remaining in the background and not participating in the ensuing conversation. He could, he thought irritably, almost hear her tapping her heels as she waited for him to conclude his pleasantries.

George was looking better than he had looked since the stroke. However much warring took place in the house, he was obviously thriving on it. His cheeks were pink and there was a general air of cheerfulness only lightly camouflaged underneath the habitual crusty exterior. Neither he nor Ellie seemed aware of this subtle change, however. Odd.

'I hate omelette,' he complained, stabbing the egg with a fork and putting some into his mouth.

'It's good for you,' Ellie said from behind James, in a brisk voice.

'So are most of those things in life not worth having, eating, doing or owning.'

'If you say so, Father.'

'You should try a few vices, my girl. Might do you some good.'

Ellie went bright red. 'I'm altogether too boring. You know that.' It was a fine return. Light and nonchalant, but underneath James was aware of some undercurrent that went beyond what had been said. And her father was clearly aware of it as well, because he stopped eating and stared at her intently.

'I take it that was meant as a joke, Eleanor,' he said seriously.

Ellie, who had gone a shade brighter, turned away and replied that it was, what she really should have said was that her timetable precluded too many vices, but she'd bear his words in mind.

James decided that he would ask her about that remark later, find out where all those discordant notes between father and daughter came from. Then he told himself that it was no concern of his, so why bother?

As soon as they were on the plane, though, he found himself asking the very question he had decided was no concern of his.

'Is this thing safe?' she answered, ignoring the question, and looking around her a little anxiously.

James looked at her with surprise. 'You're not nervous, are you?' Sitting this close to her, he could see a few fine lines around her eyes, but apart from that she looked much younger than her age. Odd, he thought, considering the stress levels of her job.

'I hope your pilot knows what he's doing.'

'So do I.' He laughed, feeling himself relax, but then he saw the worried expression on her face and added seriously, 'He's flown me a thousand times before.'

'What if he keels over?'

Did she know that when she asked questions like that, with her brow puckered into that very small frown, she looked like a child of fifteen?

'In that case, I guess you're about the most valuable passenger he could hope for.'

'And what happens to the plane in the meanwhile?' she demanded, turning to look at him so that he could see the small streaks of hazel in her crystal green eyes. 'While I'm sorting him out? Don't tell me that it'll obligingly fly itself until everything's back to normal.'

'Stop worrying. I can pilot a plane myself.'

'Are you just saying that to put my mind at rest?' Ellie asked, eyeing him suspiciously.

'Well, yes, if you must know.'

Which made her smile, tilting the corners of her mouth upwards. James looked away quickly. He had a sinking feeling that his eyes might stray from her face to the rounded outline of her breasts just visible under the cool, cotton shirt. He had no intention of inviting another of those pointed 'Quite finished?' remarks.

'I imagined,' he murmured, 'that you were too level-headed to be scared of flying.'

'I'm not scared of *flying*,' she corrected him. 'I'm just a little nervous about being in this tiny aircraft. Big planes just seem so much…'

'Bigger?' He couldn't resist it. He wasn't looking at her. In fact, he had his head back against the head-rest and his eyes were half-closed, but the temptation to feel her reaction at being teased was irresistible. He had to remind himself that giving in to this sort of temptation was really only a step away from giving in to the old curiosity thing—and everyone knew what happened to the over-curious cat.

'Very funny.'

'I don't have to see you to know that you've reverted to that tight-lipped look.' He closed his eyes and felt, insanely, like grinning. 'You still haven't told me how you're coping at the surgery.'

'It's very relaxing after hospital life,' she admitted.

Now, he thought, she's staring out of the window, probably praying for clear weather, no high winds, no unexpected flocks of birds, no sudden drops in the petrol gauge.

'And not as heart-rending,' she continued, in the same thoughtful voice. 'Dealing with sick children on a daily basis can get a little...'

'Disheartening?'

'I guess so. But the rewards are boundless.' They turned to face each other at precisely the same time and their gazes locked. 'I've started the ball rolling for a replacement. I should get some feedback on that pretty soon.'

'How very efficient.'

'That's me. Very efficient.' But she looked disconcerted at that and he felt a perverse rush of satisfaction at being able to break through some of her composure.

He wondered briefly if she was becoming one of those things which were supposed to exist—namely a challenge. God, he thought, I must be cynical, but he couldn't prevent a sudden thrill running through him and he ruefully laughed off the feeling. What next? he wondered.

'And how's your father? He says that he's been to the surgery a couple of times.'

'Yes, he has.' He heard the cautious tone in her voice

and realised that she was calculating how much she should or shouldn't tell him, and that irritated him more than it should have. What was the big secret? he wanted to ask. Did she think that he would use any information against her at a later date? Or was reticence a habit too ingrained for her to break, without thinking first about it?

'He just does bits and pieces and I always keep an eye on him.' Her voice relaxed. 'I have to keep telling him not to push himself before he's ready. I hate it, hate sounding like a nag.' She sounded defensive but slightly wounded.

'Well, your father seems to be relaxed enough, so your nagging can't be getting on his nerves that much.'

Ellie stared at him coolly. God, he hated that look. It was the sort of look that could only be erased if he either shook her or kissed her.

'I would have noticed if my father was in a better temper. I live with him. You don't. I assure you, he's as…he's the same as ever…'

'If you say so. Still, at least he reacts. That sounds a healthy enough reaction,' he commented neutrally, watching her face closely.

'I guess so…' She shrugged and looked away into the distance. 'The very worst thing a patient recovering from a stroke can do is to give up. You'd be surprised as to what the right frame of mind can achieve.'

And she rambled on about the subject while he continued to watch her covertly. Her hair was looking slightly less rigidly restrained than when they had first started out and he had an insane desire to tuck the loose strands behind her ear. He diplomatically kept his hands to himself, and when there was a pause in the conversation he said casually, 'Guess what.'

'What?'

'We didn't crash.'

She looked at him and suddenly smiled broadly.

'Didn't I tell you that it would be as safe as houses?' he asked.

'You were quite right. I'll leave my security blanket and teddy bear at home next time, shall I?'

There was the most fleeting of silences, then the moment was broken by the landing of the plane and all the fuss afterwards as they disembarked and headed towards the Jaguar waiting to chauffeur them into London.

He had to persuade her to let him drop her off directly at her house. She had, he noticed, a tendency to argue nearly every point, but he found himself more than willing to argue back. The women he had dated in the past had never argued with him. Was there such a thing as too obliging? he wondered.

'So,' he said casually as she was leaving the car, 'plans for the day?'

Ellie, busy retrieving her bag, wasn't looking at him. He followed her with his eyes, and when she bent down to fetch her handbag from the seat he noticed the swell of her breasts pushing against her shirt and became aware of that sensation again, of being sixteen once more, with sexy thoughts in his head.

'Oh, hospital and more hospital,' she said, pulling out of the car, straightening, then leaning to peer at him through the car window. 'Thanks very much for the lift. It was extremely useful.'

'What do you say to an early supper this evening? Before you leave?' I can't believe I just asked that, he thought to himself.

'That's very kind of you,' Ellie told him, her cheeks pink, 'but I'm afraid I've made other plans.'

He hadn't expected her to accept. He had known, even as he'd uttered the invitation, that she was going to make up some excuse to turn him down, even if that meant out-and-out lying. So why the hell had he asked in the first place? I must be a damned masochist, he thought angrily.

'Sure.'

'Henry's coming over for supper.'

Was it his imagination, or was there an element of kindness in her voice when she said that? He could barely look at her, he suddenly felt so enraged. He managed to mutter something along the lines of 'Have a good time', and bared his teeth in something that was a caricature of a smile.

When the car pulled away, he made a great show of opening his briefcase and poring over his documents, but he could see Vince, his chauffeur, flicking glances at him in the rear-view mirror and he had to resist the temptation to tell him to get on with the driving and mind his own damned business.

Politely turned down by a woman. He decided that it had been the politeness, the *kindness* in her voice when she had rejected his invitation that had really got his goat.

By six o'clock he was in no mood to continue at the office, and even though he had a little black book, with numbers of some very charming women, all now friends, some married, and all of whom would have loved to see him, he still couldn't make his mind up what to do. He sat in his penthouse apartment overlooking Regent's Park and contemplated the black book with a certain degree of loathing.

There was nothing to be said for a woman treating you as though you were a poisonous reptile. Especially when you'd gone out of your way to be *nice*, for heaven's sake.

Henry was clearly a martyr. Or possibly a madman.

James strolled through the apartment, pausing to glance at the view, though not taking it in.

It might, he conceded, be amusing just to pop over to

her place, if only to catch a glimpse of the remarkable Henry. A flying visit, so to speak. He'd stay literally five minutes. After all, he reasoned, what was the point of indulging in curiosity if you made no attempt to satisfy it? Besides, it would be informative to find out just how seriously she was involved with this Henry chap. After all, he could prove a stumbling block when it came to her commitment to the surgery, couldn't he?

She was entitled to her private life, James thought magnanimously, but she would have to put it on hold at least for the time being. Henry would have to contain any possessive instincts he might have. Yes, a surprise visit would definitely be educational.

He paused long enough to have a quick shower and change into something less formal—a pair of beige trousers, a cream shirt and a cream fisherman-style jumper—then he was out of the house. Feeling refreshed, invigorated and nicely anticipatory.

It was only when he was standing in front of Ellie's door, with his hand poised to ring the bell, that he wondered whether this impromptu visit was really such a good idea.

Too late for such concerns now, he thought logically. For a start, the taxi's gone.

He pressed the buzzer, stood back and shoved his hands in his pockets. Although the curtains had been drawn, the lights were on, so there was someone there. And, sure enough, the door opened and there she was, dressed in jeans and a jumper, an expression of first surprise, then alarm, on her face.

'What are you doing here?'

Put like that, James suddenly didn't know. He really had no idea. He also couldn't think of anything sensible to say by way of a response.

'Don't look so overjoyed,' he muttered, and she reluctantly stood aside so that he could enter.

'I wasn't expecting you.' She looked up at him, then glanced over her shoulder towards the kitchen.

'No. Well, I happened to be passing through this area...' I risk, James thought acidly, becoming somewhat ridiculous. Traipsing over here for no possible reason and then fabricating the most clichéd of excuses for dropping by. 'Went to visit a client who lives near here...'

'Oh, really? Where?' He could tell that she was hardly thinking about what she was saying, because her eyes kept flicking between him and the kitchen. It occurred to him that she was probably trying to stall him out here for a few minutes until she could think of a good excuse to get rid of him, while Henry remained tucked away behind closed doors in the kitchen.

'Swiss Cottage,' James said abruptly. 'I could do with a drink.' The realisation that she was trying to get rid of him, and not very subtly either, had the opposite effect on him. Instead of being anxious to leave, he now felt an irrational desire to stay. For as long as possible.

An expression of resignation crossed her face and she nodded in the direction of the kitchen.

'Henry and I were just about to have a bite in the kitchen. Do join us, although there may not be an awful lot to go round.'

'Henry's here?' James contrived to look startled, embarrassed and taken aback all at once.

'Yes.' Ellie turned and frowned thoughtfully. 'I thought I mentioned that to you this morning.'

'Possibly. Can't remember.' He followed her towards the kitchen. 'I wouldn't like to be in the way of... anything...'

She didn't answer. Just pushed open the kitchen door to reveal a tall, slimmish, very pleasant-looking chap with brown hair who was standing stirring something in a frying-pan. His face was flushed from the heat and as soon as he looked up and saw them he smiled and said cheerfully, 'Damned hard work, all this cooking...'

He extended his hand to James, who shook it briefly while Ellie rattled off an introduction then proceeded to survey the scene with his hands in his pockets.

And what a little scene of joyful domesticity it was, he thought sourly. Matching aprons appeared to be the only things missing. He wished to God he hadn't come.

'Sit down, old man,' Henry said, glancing over his shoulder as he rummaged through the cupboards and began extracting dishes and crockery.

'Thanks,' James said. 'Old man.' This elicited a sharp look from Ellie and no response at all from Henry, who was too busy doing his own thing. 'So, Ellie tells me that you're a doctor.' James then proceeded to sit back and observe while Henry took up the cue and launched into a monologue on his profession.

Nice enough, James decided after ten minutes, but a bore. Over the meal, he tried to catch Ellie's eye, but she refused to look in his direction. He was, he concluded, intrigued by precisely what lay between her and Henry. Couldn't she see for herself that the man lacked any semblance of excitement?

Which was obviously why they were so well suited. A career woman like herself, immersed in a job that took up most of her time, certainly didn't need to arrive back at her apartment, exhausted, only to be confronted by excitement.

After all, he thought, it's hardly as though *she's* the most invigorating person in the universe.

That thought made him smile. It also made him feel slightly superior.

Yes, they deserved one another. They probably discussed medical matters when they were together, mused over the *Doctor's Weekly*, or whatever else it was that doctors were supposed to bone up on. He couldn't en-

visage Henry flying into a rage if his girlfriend, for want
of a better word, told him that she might have to be out
of London for some time. He looked the sort who took
refuge in the steady drip of grumbling rather than an
almighty explosion.

They finished eating and while Ellie cleared the
kitchen they were dismissed into the small sitting room
to await cups of coffee.

Henry's face was flushed and he was beaming rather
a lot.

'Don't normally drink too much,' Henry said, inter-
preting James's expression correctly. 'But tonight's
something special.'

They sat down and James wondered whether he would
be privy to some exciting news. Perhaps there had been
a breakthrough in the cure of athlete's foot.

'Really?'

Ellie walked in with a tray, distributed coffee and then
sat next to Henry on the sofa. She was wearing her hair
tied back in a French pleat and she pulled it over one
shoulder and toyed with the ends, curling the fine,
blonde hair around her fingers. James tore his eyes away
from the spectacle and said, settling back into his chair,
'And what's so special about tonight, Henry? Old man?'

Ellie frowned at him again, as he'd known she would,
and he flashed her a beaming smile and sipped some of
his coffee.

'Shall we tell all, Ells?' They exchanged a look and
curiously, James thought, Ellie suddenly looked girlishly
embarrassed.

He crossed his legs and raised his eyebrows with polite curiosity.

Definitely suited, he thought. They might even have
his and hers matching dressing gowns and bath towels.
He wondered briefly what Ellie would look like in a

dressing gown, then found his mind straying to more vivid pictures of what she would look like without one.

He quickly switched off that line of thought, although he was disconcerted to find that his skin felt hot and he had stiffened slightly under his zip.

'You can't keep me in suspense with all this,' he said quickly, throwing them both a smile that was now feeling forced.

'Henry,' Ellie said—was there, James thought, a little edge of desperation in her voice?—'I really think…'

'Heck, Ells,' Henry said a little loudly, 'I can't keep this to myself.' He looked at James, except, after several glasses of wine, he seemed to peer in an owl-like fashion. 'You're the first to know, James. Ellie and I are engaged.'

Silence. It seemed to stretch quite a while and James continued to smile. Unless he said something soon he knew that the silence would exceed the bounds of comfort and start to get embarrassing.

'Congratulations!' He raised his coffee cup. 'We really need some champagne on an occasion like this!' Well, this, he thought, changes *everything*.

'Or at least…' Henry said, gazing at Ellie in what James now realised was a drunken stupor. Did the man have *no* self control? 'Or at least the time to consume it?'

'Of course,' James said, looking at Ellie with the same smile on his face. 'What time does your plane leave?'

'I haven't been able to get a flight for this evening,' she admitted guiltily. She looked between them. 'Left it too late, I guess. I've arranged for Mrs Cribb to stay the night with Father.'

'In which case,' Henry shouted merrily, 'let's celebrate!'

Ellie was looking nervous at what James suspected cynically was wild and unnatural behaviour for Henry.

'Yes, why don't we?' he said, feeling it necessary to show some male support.

'Because,' Ellie said, standing up, 'I'm exhausted. I had planned on having an early night... I think it's time for both of you to leave... Anyway, Henry...' She looked at Henry and sighed. 'How much have you had to drink?'

'Oh, leave the poor chap alone!' James interjected with ferocious good humour, and Ellie threw him a dark look from under her lashes which he blithely ignored.

'Haven't you got somewhere to go?' she asked with saccharine sweetness. 'A meeting? An appointment? A date of some description?'

I was right, James thought. Poor old Henry. One lapse from his normal stable, predictable behaviour, and she jumps down his throat. Couldn't he see that the only marriage that would ever suit Eleanor Mills was one that involved her career? How could he fail to notice that domineering streak in her?

'Nothing on the horizon,' he assured her with a smile, following them both to the door.

'Henry, are you quite sure you don't want me to call a taxi for you?' She looked at him anxiously and in the background James could feel himself fighting to control a scowl. How on earth could the poor man not see that this marriage business had all the potential makings of a nightmare? Not that they weren't suited, he thought, but now that he had seen them in action it was clear that any such suitability was purely superficial.

Henry was shaking his head vigorously. He had gone red in the face and looked as though he might teeter over.

'The walk to the underground'll do me a world of good, darling.' He bent down and planted a chaste kiss on Ellie's lips, and James could see a pinkish colour crawl up her neck as she briefly returned the kiss.

That was the problem with women like her, he thought ferociously. They blushed just enough to make you think that they were vulnerable, but any fool could see that underneath they were barracudas.

As soon as Henry had gone, Ellie turned to him and folded her arms.

'Did you bring a coat?' she asked meaningfully, and James responded by heading back towards the sitting room.

It was clear now, he thought paternally, what he had to do. He had to have a serious yet tactful chat with her about this marriage thing. After all, someone had to remind her that her responsibilities lay elsewhere at the moment. She really could not go all gooey-eyed simply because there was a ring on the appropriate finger—that would be a disaster. Whatever she might believe, her father needed her with him at the moment and the surgery needed her skills.

And, anyway, were those two *really* suited? Of course, that was entirely incidental, but how would he feel if they launched themselves into wedlock, only to discover heartbreak a few years down the line?

He sat down, while Ellie fumed in silence for a few seconds by the sitting-room door, then he said quite calmly, 'Any chance of another cup of coffee?'

CHAPTER FIVE

'ANOTHER cup of coffee?' Ellie echoed behind him. *'Another cup of coffee?'*

'Yes, thanks.' James settled himself onto the sofa, folded his arms and looked at her impassively.

Ellie looked back at him, not wanting to, but unable to stop herself. She could feel her heart beating feverishly, even though the rest of her body felt like lead. Had Cameron Clark made her feel like this? She could hardly remember. Odd the way that brief, intense fling had felt so real at the time, yet now she could hardly recall the details. She certainly couldn't remember ever having this suffocating feeling back then. A dawning awareness, perhaps, that she and Cameron were not suited, a gradual awakening to the reality that physical attraction did not necessarily go hand in hand with a successful relationship. She lowered her eyes, resisting the compulsion to look at James.

She fiddled with the engagement ring on her finger with a certain amount of relief. It seemed the only safe thing in her life at the moment, when everything else was shifting in perspective. Dear Henry, the steady rock.

She raised her eyes and allowed James a tight, polite smile.

'A quick cup, then.'

How, she thought, baffled, could someone as competent and self-confident as she was in her career flounder so comprehensively when it came to her emotions? The ring on her finger felt like an anchor in a storm.

She returned to the sitting room, handed him a mug, sat down and yawned dramatically.

'Big day?' he asked casually. 'How was the hospital?'

'Is that why you stayed for another cup of coffee? So that you could enquire about my day?'

He shrugged, but since he seemed to be waiting for an answer Ellie obligingly gave him an abbreviated version of what she had done at the hospital, then politely asked him about his day.

'Meetings!' He grimaced ruefully. 'The bane of the businessman's life.'

'Especially one who runs so many businesses single-handedly.'

'Especially…' He sipped some coffee and then cradled the mug in his hands. 'Nice to meet Henry, put a face to the name.'

Ellie didn't say anything. Where was this leading to? James's questions, she was fast discovering, always led to something.

'He seems a pleasant enough chap,' he continued.

'Oh, I'm so glad you've seen fit to pass him!' She smiled coolly. 'I shall sleep easier tonight.'

'They say that sarcasm is a defence mechanism for keeping people at arm's length.'

'Oh, do they?' Ellie raised her eyebrows in a show of interest at that.

'Yes, they do. You don't want me to ask you about him, do you?'

'Hurry up and drink your coffee.' She tried another convincing yawn, but this time it failed to work—probably, she thought, because his presence was making her too tense.

She looked at him, all shadows and angles, and felt a fierce jolt of confusion and excitement. What *was* it about him? It couldn't just be his looks. He was not the first good-looking man she had ever met in her life. Nor could it be his wealth and power. Those things, she had heard, could be potent aphrodisiacs, but they had never

impressed her. Ill health was a great leveller and a hospital was one of the few places where money and status
ceased to be of importance.

It was true that he could be quite witty, in a dry,
charming way, but then so could lots of men. If she
needed dry wit she could turn on the television and be
lulled by any number of dry, witty stand-up comedians,
without having to endure all the complicated, soul-
searching baggage that came with it.

So what was it? A combination of all those things?
She wished that she could work it out, like all those
mathematical puzzles which she could solve with no difficulty at all. She wished she could put her finger on it.
She wished that she could stop her breath from catching
in her throat every time she looked at him.

Instead, she continually felt as though her façade of
cool control was being sabotaged.

'How long have you two known each other?'

'Ah. So that's what this is all leading to...a cross-
examination on Henry—though I haven't got the faintest
idea what concern it is of yours.'

'Haven't you?' He gave her a long, cool scrutiny
which very nearly bordered on rude. 'Then I'll get right
to the point, shall I? This engagement of yours comes
at a very bad time. I had no idea that you and this Henry
chap were so close.'

Ellie's mouth dropped open. Was she hearing correctly? Maybe if she hopped up and down on one foot
and shook her head at the same time his words would
take on a different meaning.

'You're not telling me that I ought to ask your permission before I get engaged, are you?' She gave an
incredulous little laugh and James's lips thinned.

'I'm telling you that your father needs you at the moment. I can only assume that Henry has put that ring on

your finger in an attempt to persuade you to come back to London.'

'Henry did not *put* that ring on my finger! Could you please credit me with a mind?'

'Women have an annoying habit of losing all contact with rational thought the minute wedding bells start ringing in the distance...'

'What?' She folded her arms and glared at him with hostility. 'A couple of days ago, I was the epitome of the hard-headed career woman. Now suddenly I'm an irrational little fool whose brain has been scrambled by a ring on my finger? Which is it?'

'You're overreacting.'

'*I'm* overreacting? You come to my house uninvited, and then proceed to give me a lecture on how to run my life! Are you really surprised that I'm a little put out?' Wasn't this precisely the sort of man she loathed? A man who gave orders and volunteered his opinions whether or not they were asked for? She tried to think of Henry, to conjure up his easygoing, amiable face, but she couldn't. Every bit of her mind was filled to overflowing with James Kellern. There was no room left for anyone else.

'Also, I have to tell you that I think you and Henry are totally unsuitable as marriage partners.' He stared at her, unruffled.

She could feel her face growing hotter and hotter. How dare you? she wanted to yell. I'm thirty-four years old, I'm a highly qualified doctor. I am not a complete idiot! She opened her mouth but nothing came out.

'I—I happen to be very fond of Henry,' she stuttered furiously. 'Not that it's any of your business. We get along. I realise that probably doesn't fit in with your definition of why two people should get married, but there's more to our relationship than thunder and lightning and the earth moving. What we have is something deeper, something built to last. Trust, friendship—qual-ities that are the backbone of a good marriage.' She wanted to repeat this over and over like a mantra because it stabilised her, and she hadn't realised quite how much she needed stability in her life until James Kellern had entered it.

Good marriages weren't built on wild highs and lows, on agony and ecstasy. They weren't built on the ebb and flow of the unpredictable. *Contentment* wasn't built on the ebb and flow of the unpredictable. She hadn't been content since she had returned to Ireland to help her father. Everything had been turned upside down. Her feelings about her home, about her father, about the na-ture and quality of her life in London. She wished she could yell at him that she wanted her contentment *back* and being engaged to Henry would achieve that.

'You make it all sound like a business arrangement,' James remarked neutrally. 'Are you in love with him?'

Ellie didn't answer. Eventually she said coldly, 'Were you in love with your wife?'

'Clearly not. Or maybe I should say clearly not enough. Considering she now lives halfway across the world and I'm more than happy with the situation.'

'Henry and I are extremely well suited.' She glared at him, but somehow still felt compelled to continue her self-defence. 'It's never easy being married to a doctor. He understands. He doesn't object when the phone rings and I have to vanish at three in the morning because there's an emergency. He doesn't moan when I have to cancel things at the last minute.'

'Obliging.'

'Yes. Extremely!' Ellie informed him shortly, hearing the implicit sarcasm in his voice and reacting to it.

She was getting more and more flustered. A few weeks ago, James Kellern had simply been a name in her head, a vague memory of someone who had inhabited the same part of the planet as herself. Now he was a presence that she couldn't seem to shake off.

'And what about excitement? What about the thrill of passion?'

'What about it?' She blushed and looked away. 'There's excitement. There's passion.' She hoped that her brief interlude of silence would be enough for him to assume that she was telling the truth, that modesty prevented her from going into detail. So what did it matter if Henry wasn't the most passionate person on the face of the earth? Neither, for that matter, was she. She had had one glimpse of excitement years ago and had found it not to her liking.

'More importantly, Henry happens to be a very nice, reliable, dependable...' she rooted around for a few more adjectives '...man. He would make anyone a wonderful husband.' Ellie looked at the hard, masculine face with its uncompromising lines and said defiantly, 'I can see that you're not listening to a word I'm saying! So what sort of man would you prescribe for me? A lout? An unreliable, irresponsible cad? Someone who spends his time making macho remarks and shouting orders for his dinner?'

She could see his mouth quivering. He looked as though he was about to grin, and that infuriated her further. He was the one, after all, who had initiated the stupid discussion. The least he could do was treat her remarks seriously. If he weren't so big, so powerful, she might even have considered physically dragging him to the door and chucking him out.

'That's going to a ludicrous extreme,' James remarked impatiently. 'I'm merely saying that I think you're far too strong for a man like Henry. Whether he admits it openly to you or not, he needs a woman who's going to bear him a few children and be content to remain in the background, supporting him emotionally.'

For some reason, that hurt. He made her sound like a tyrant. Did he think that she kept a set of chains in the broom cupboard? To be pulled out whenever the occasion demanded?

'I'm very supportive,' Ellie muttered. Her voice sounded thin and she cleared her throat and looked across at him. 'He's always been able to rely on me for that.'

James shook his head impatiently and stood up. She watched as he restlessly prowled the room, hands in pockets. 'You'll end up walking all over him,' he said abruptly, pausing to stand in front of her so that she reluctantly had to look up at him. 'If you don't already. Where's the challenge in that sort of relationship?' He leant over and rested his hands on the sides of her chair and involuntarily she cringed back, overwhelmed by a feeling of suffocation.

Her body was tense, as though every nerve-ending had frozen in alarm at his proximity. When he straightened up, she could feel herself sag with relief.

'How many men have you ever been out with?'

'You're out of line with this questioning, James Kellern! You've said what you had to say on the subject of my fiancé.' She had very nearly, she thought, stammered over that word and was pleased that she hadn't. 'You certainly don't need to continue any further!'

'I'm not interested in how many men you've slept with...I'm just asking how many men you've ever dated. How many women, for that matter, has Henry been out with? If you two have known each other from medical college?'

'You don't need to try every field to know that the one you're standing on is green enough,' Ellie muttered mutinously.

She hated the way he could expose her like this, hold those vulnerable bits up to her like a mirror when she would rather not have seen them at all, make her feel like an awkward child, make her forget where her strengths were.

'Oh, for God's sake, woman! You need someone as strong as yourself.'

There you go again, she wanted to shout. *I'm not strong!* But I *am*, she thought in confusion. No one could accuse her of *not* being strong. Could they?

'I don't,' she said, with a lot more vigour than she felt. 'I don't need someone strong and if that's your diagnosis of the situation then you're completely wide of the mark. What I need is someone who relaxes me. I come home drained at night. I don't want a man who's just going to add to the situation and I don't need a man who's going to complain if I don't immediately want to don the glad rags and go out dancing.'

I sound as though I should be attached to a Zimmer frame, she thought despairingly. This is coming out all wrong. She looked at that dark, shuttered face and wondered how he could make her feel so bewildered by a situation that was, when you got down to it, really very simple.

'You told me your wife was a career woman and that what you look for in the female sex is a woman who's uncluttered. Perhaps I need the male equivalent. Anyway, Henry happens to be very intelligent. It just so happens that he's affable and good-natured with it. I consider myself very lucky. I guess I must just be a very boring person.' She half smiled and James stood up abruptly, raking his fingers through his hair.

Now, with the uncomfortable conversation clearly at an end, she didn't know whether she was disappointed or relieved.

'In that case, I offer you my most sincere congratulations.' He walked towards the door and she followed him. 'But,' he asked, turning to face her with one hand on the doorknob, 'does he turn you on?'

The directness of the question was unexpected enough to make the colour rush to her face. His voice was soft and idle and it wrapped itself around her, seeping through the pores of her skin, turning her blood to lava.

'I expect you'll tell me that it's none of my business,' he murmured, pre-emptying her reply. 'Or maybe you can't possibly answer because you're exhausted and you need to get to sleep...'

'Y-yes—yes, of course he turns me on,' Ellie stammered. Her eyes travelled upwards to his face and remained there, locked by some terrible, overpowering magnetic pull that made her breathing ragged.

'I'm glad to hear it.' He was still staring at her and the atmosphere was charged with a peculiar undercurrent of unspoken words. What words, though? What words? She hardly knew what she was thinking. She only knew that this was a moment of time which she had to dispel.

'So,' she said, stepping back and blinking hard, 'I shall probably see you some time when you return to Ireland.'

'I expect so.'

'What plans do you have for tomorrow?' If my voice gets any more brittle, she thought, it'll shatter into a thousand pieces, like a glass bauble.

'Usual series of meetings.' He shrugged and opened the door, and the mood was broken. She watched him leave and then locked the door, just in case he decided to reappear with another barrage of clever insights.

The problem with James Kellern, she thought later, after she had packed two suitcases with clothes and a few medical books, was that he represented the unknown and the unpredictable. He was an uncontrollable force and he seemed to turn her into one as well, whenever he was with her. She didn't want her life to be out of control. She liked to see its horizons, because its horizons were her safety.

Henry she could fathom. And even if she had only known him for five minutes she would still be able to fathom him. There were no hidden depths there, or at least none that had ever made themselves known to her. No dark corners that remained to be explored.

Henry was restful. Excitement was one thing, she thought, but as a daily diet it would get a little too much. She wished that she had thought of using this argument when James had thrown his clever little remarks at her. She wished that she had been more articulate, more coherent, that her mind had been able to function lucidly, instead of being wrapped up in cotton wool.

She was far more lucky the following day, when she sat down with her father after dinner and broke the news of her engagement to him.

'Getting married, eh?' He gave her one of those reducing looks. 'Wondered when you'd get around to it.'

'Did you think that I'd end up on the shelf?'

'Thought you were married to your work.'

Here we go again, Ellie thought. Have I disappointed him again? 'I won't be giving up my job, Father.'

'No.' He paused and looked at her with quiet curiosity. 'I can't picture you with an apron tied round your waist and several children dangling from it.'

Ellie felt her breathing quicken. Dammit, her eyes seemed to be filling up. Again. What was it with this place? She seemed to spend her whole time here on the verge of tears, for whatever reason.

'You were always aggressive, even when you were a child,' he mused, and she thought bitterly, Well, wasn't that what you wanted? Everyone seemed to think so. You wanted a son and the best I could do was turn myself into the female equivalent. 'Head in your books. No time for dolls and baking cakes.'

'You never gave me any dolls, Father. How was I expected to play with them?'

He looked startled at this response, and frankly she felt rather startled by it as well. Were they *talking*? She couldn't remember the last time they had *talked*.

'I wanted to get you one for your birthday,' he told her. 'Fifth birthday. Went to one of those toy stores but I ended up with an armful of books instead. Your mother…'

'She wasn't there, Father. You should have bought that doll.' Now she felt as though her entire future had depended on the purchase of a doll from a toy store. Instead of books, books and more books, all educational. By the age of nine, she'd known nothing about pretend cooking or pretend housekeeping or pretend mothers, but she'd known a great deal about weather patterns, tropical rain forests and the basics of the human body.

She stood up and began clearing the dishes.

'And who's the lucky chap?'

Ellie didn't want to talk about Henry. She wanted to carry on talking about that non-existent doll that could have changed the course of her life. She wanted to hang onto that personal snatch of conversation and keep it going.

'Another doctor. A GP. His name's Henry.' She efficiently washed the dishes, then sat back down at the kitchen table with two cups of coffee. 'He's very kind and thoughtful. Father, tell me something. How did you feel when you and Mother were about to get married? Were you excited?'

It would be par for the course, she knew, if he refused to answer that one. But she was going to be here for a while and the time was coming when barriers would have to be climbed, if they weren't to coexist in polite silence.

'Odd kind of question, my girl,' he said eventually,

with enough caution in his voice to show her that his thoughts were along the same lines as hers. 'Why do you ask?'

'Because I'm interested.' She sighed. 'I'm thirty-four years old and in all that time you've never once spoken about my mother.' Now that she had started she realised that she had to go on. It was like jumping through a ring of fire, hoping against hope that you came out in one piece on the other side.

'I have no real idea what she was like. There aren't even very many photos. I need to know. Please tell me. Were you happy together?' She was clutching the handle of the cup and she realised, with dismay, that she was already anticipating a lack of response. It occurred to her that that had been the story of her life. A nervous anticipation of her father's displeasure. But if James Kellern had got through to him, then why not her? She might not be a man, but she was his *daughter*, for God's sake. His own flesh and blood!

'I can't think what's got into you,' her father said, looking at her sharply, but for once Ellie refused to scuttle away, back into silence.

'Curiosity, Father. It's always been there, believe it or not, but I'm only now giving it a voice.'

'Yes, of course we were happy,' he said, his tone blustery. She remained silent, waiting for him to continue, refusing to give him a way out. 'I remember being very excited about getting married. Knew it was the right thing. We both did.'

'Did you?' She fiddled with her engagement ring and thought of Henry, realising, as she did so, that she was thinking along the lines of a sheet of paper, split into two columns: 'for' and 'against'. It occurred to her that people who were sure that they were doing the right thing wouldn't approach the situation in quite the same manner. She had accepted the ring the way a drowning swimmer clutched a lifebelt, because her emotions had been in a state of turmoil and that ring represented the comfort of safety. Time was playing its tricks now, though, forcing her to think.

'Never any doubt. She was a good woman, your mother. Warm, kind, funny. Broke my heart when she died—I don't have to tell you that. Never could replace her, you know, because she was irreplaceable.' He stood up. 'Now, Eleanor, enough of that.' His eyes looked watery, and she allowed him to shuffle into the sitting room.

Later, she brought him his cup of cocoa and they sat together watching television, in silence.

'When does this young man of yours plan on coming over?' he asked as he was about to retire to bed, and Ellie gave it some thought. 'What about next weekend?' her father suggested. 'I don't think,' he continued with a rare foray into humour, 'that I have to consult my hectic social calendar to know that we have nothing planned.'

'Next weekend it is, in that case,' Ellie agreed.

So now it was no longer just the ring on her finger and the vaguest of notions that marriage was looming somewhere on the horizon. Henry was coming over to meet her father, to get the paternal stamp of approval.

It was agreed, when she telephoned him, that he would travel up next Friday, arriving in time for supper. And on that afternoon she found herself racing around the shops, returning home with two carrier bags full of food, which she laboriously set to work at transforming into a three-course meal.

Her father, for want of anything better to do, hovered in the background until she eventually gave him salad ingredients to chop, a task which he attacked with such mathematical precision that the exercise took him ten times longer than it would have taken her.

'We should have asked James Kellern across,' he observed somewhere along the line, and since it was too late Ellie magnanimously agreed, shrugging her shoulders in simulated regret.

Asked James Kellern across? Not on your life. She had neither seen nor heard from him since she had arrived back from London, and had decided that she could almost begin to put him in perspective if he obligingly kept out of her way for the remainder of her time in Ireland.

She certainly wasn't going to be requesting the pleasure of his company—least of all when Henry was around. He had made his views on Henry quite clear and she had no intention of seeing him in action again, when he would no doubt go to great lengths to make his point. Oh, no.

Let her father see Henry without prejudice. He was certain to like him. Everyone liked Henry—it was virtually impossible not to.

And he did. As it turned out, Henry got off to a good start by appearing with a bottle of vintage port, a drink her father was very partial to, and the fact that they were in the same profession proved fertile conversational ground. They chatted quite harmoniously.

In fact, over the main course, Ellie relaxed and found herself listening to them, observing Henry and mentally going through her list of pros and cons. Again.

Yes, Henry really was a very nice man. They really were suited, weren't they? And if James Kellern had quite a bit to say on the matter, then that was his concern.

'I like your father,' Henry told her when they were alone in the kitchen afterwards, washing the dishes, and she almost said in response that, yes, he had been rather likeable, hadn't he?

And the following morning her father said precisely

the same thing about Henry; that he was a very likeable chap.

It was only later in the day that he dropped the bombshell, when the three of them were in the sitting room, reading several newspapers, doing the crosswords and browsing through a few medical journals.

'Thought you young people might like to have some fun tonight,' her father said out of the blue, and Ellie looked at him, startled.

'After all,' he continued, now that he had gained their attention, 'you don't want to be cooped up with an old man for company again. Should take Henry out to see the sights in Dublin, Eleanor.'

'I don't know any sights in Dublin,' she pointed out. 'I suppose we could all go out for a nice meal somewhere…' She racked her brains and tried to think of a restaurant, but could only come up with the one that James had taken her to. Which was *not* on the cards, just in case it was a frequent haunt of his and he happened to be there.

'What do you two get up to in London?' her father asked, putting aside the newspaper and gathering momentum for this line of conversation. He would never normally have asked her a question like that, she realised. Having Henry around clearly gave him a certain amount of bravado, and this in turn made her wonder whether all those years of stilted communication hadn't partly been her fault. Was she off-putting? James had pretty much said so. Was it also her father's opinion?

Henry looked at Ellie and she looked at him, and eventually she said, rather lamely, 'Well, when we manage to get our schedules to coincide, we usually just stay in, or else we go out for a meal.'

'When I was your age,' her father announced reminiscently, 'your mother and I used to paint the town red.

Which is what I've arranged for you and Henry to do tonight.'

'Arranged?' *You used to paint the town red?* What a day for revelations!

Her father nodded. 'I gave James a call and he'll be coming round to fetch the two of you around eight-thirty tonight. Told him to show you both the nightlife.'

'Oh, God,' Ellie said, dismayed.

'Really?' Henry was looking interested in the idea. 'Haven't been to a nightclub for the longest while. Might be fun.'

'I knew you'd like the idea.' Her father gazed at both of them in satisfaction. 'We can have a nice little meal together, then you two can go out and enjoy yourselves.' At which point he returned to the newspaper, leaving them to contemplate this *fait accompli*.

A worse idea, Ellie thought, it would have been impossible to hit upon. She didn't want to go anywhere with James Kellern, least of all to a nightclub, and she had no idea what had possessed her father to arrange such a thing in the first place. What on earth had got into him? His role in her life had always been one of minimum interference. Now here he was, sorting out her social life on her behalf.

She wondered whether she would have grimly refused to go along with the plan if there had been the smallest show of support from Henry. But there he was, back at the crossword, and this time there was a smile on his lips.

The rest of the day seemed to drag. She prepared an early supper and tried to fake high spirits over the meal, but her heart wasn't in it. All she could see in her mind's eye was James arriving sharply at eight-thirty, on his errand of mercy.

'Did you ever stop to wonder whether James had other plans?' she asked her father hopefully, and both men looked at her in astonishment at the abrupt introduction of her thoughts into the conversation.

'He was delighted at the prospect of showing you two something of the city,' her father replied, frowning.

'I hope you didn't force him into anything,' Ellie persisted. 'Perhaps—' she tested the water '—I ought to telephone him and cancel.'

'Nonsense,' her father said, and that was the end of that.

So at a little after eight she retired to her bedroom, and there began to scan her wardrobe for something suitable to wear.

Anything will do, she grumbled to herself, but nevertheless she eventually chose the only smart thing she had, in black.

James had already arrived by the time she finished her bath—a very leisurely one, because she was determined to get herself into a relaxed frame of mind—and changed into her outfit.

The dress was short and sleeveless. Normally, she wore it with something underneath, a top of some description, and a black blazer, which, combined, reduced it to something quite acceptably elegant. Tonight, on the spur of the moment, she decided to wear nothing underneath, and slung several strands of costume jewellery round her neck. With high black shoes and her hair brushed until it shone and left loose, she realised that the impression was completely different.

This will shock Henry, she thought with a grin, and realised that in fact she was thinking of James's reaction.

She heard them talking in the sitting room before she entered, and when she walked in they all fell silent. So this, she mused, is what it feels like to stage an entrance. She had seen other women do it, at a couple of medical parties in the past. Young, pretty nurses who waltzed into a crowded room, wearing next to nothing, halting the flow of the conversation.

Ellie herself had never felt in the least tempted to play those games. Clothes, as far as she was concerned, had their function, but she, personally, preferred to be seen as smartly attired rather than seductively dressed.

Now, with three pairs of eyes on her, she wondered whether this had always been the right approach. She dutifully kept her eyes on Henry, but she could feel James's grey ones on her, roving the length of her body. She wished she could see herself through his eyes. Was he impressed with her appearance, or did he think her laughable?

Henry was the first to break the silence, moving to her side, and then her father spoke. Finally James strolled towards them, hands in his pockets.

On the way to the car, he murmured into her ear, 'Very sexy. You'd better not let on to anyone that you're in charge of the surgery here. They'll be queuing to avail themselves of the service.'

'Ha, ha,' Ellie murmured back, but the compliment made her feel hot and immensely pleased.

The nightclub turned out to be down a side-street, and it was more of a jazz club than anything else. Dark, intimate, but plush, with tables set around a dance floor and a live band playing on a small, raised podium on one side.

And it was obviously very popular. The bar was crowded, even though there was waiter service at the tables, and the dance floor was packed.

Lots of well-dressed men and women, with no element of the rowdiness Ellie associated with nightclubs. She decided, as they sat down at one of the tables, that she could put up with this after all, especially since Henry was there as a buffer, so that she needn't actually address James on a one-to-one basis at all. Anyway, the music was loud enough to prohibit intimate conversation, and she was just about beginning to relax when they were descended upon by a group of people. Two men and five women, laughing, talkative, merry but not drunk.

And, of course, they all seemed to know James very well. The women, who all seemed cloned along the lines of long, silky hair and long, fluid bodies in short, figure-hugging dresses, giggled quite a bit and flirted outrageously with him.

Were these the only women he ever surrounded himself with? she thought uncharitably.

One of them, with long, dark hair and a very tight red dress, seemed to have cornered Henry. By the time the group dispersed, Ellie realised that he had been absorbed into the crowd and was on the dance floor with the leggy brunette.

'You didn't tell me that we were going to be in a group,' Ellie said to James, who was now the only one left at the table with her.

To make himself better heard, he slipped into the chair next to hers and leaned towards her, with one elbow on the table and his chin in his hands.

'Actually,' he told her, 'I had arranged to have dinner with four of that lot—Paul, Mike and their partners—and then come here afterwards.'

'So in other words you cancelled your dinner out so that you could treat Henry and me to a night of fun instead of being holed up in Father's house?'

'Do I sense a little self-righteous rage in the making?'

'Did my father force you into this?'

'No.' He looked at her directly in the eyes and for just a moment she was lost for words. The music seemed to stop, the people froze, everything went silent except for the sound of her heart beating wildly inside her.

Then he looked away to the dance floor and things

returned to normal. 'Aren't you having a good time?' he asked. 'Henry certainly seems to be.'

Ellie looked across to where Henry certainly seemed to be having a very good time indeed, dancing with quite a bit of uncoordinated abandon, in fact.

'Seems to be quite the party animal, once he's in his stride.' James's voice was mild, disarming, but she looked at him sharply, sensing rather than hearing something beneath the casual words.

'This is the first time I've seen him so…animated,' she said, for want of a better description, and James turned to look at her again.

'Everyone has their hidden side, though, don't you think?' He reached out to her and took her hand in his, and for a split second she thought…what? That he was about to ask her something about *her* hidden side?

'Would you like to dance?' He pulled her to her feet. 'No good just sitting here on the sidelines.' He leaned down and added, with a low laugh, 'After all, I did promise your father that I'd make sure you enjoyed yourself.'

CHAPTER SIX

'GOOD job I found you, wasn't it, James? What were you thinking of, taking Monty out?'

James didn't answer. He eased himself gently away from Frank, his estate manager, and managed to arrange himself on the bed.

Personally, he didn't think it *was* a good thing that Frank had discovered him, lying in an ignominious heap in a ditch with his clothes plastered to his body from the sudden downpour, aching in places he hadn't previously known existed. He would much rather have remained where he was, soaked to the skin, until the pain had worn off.

'Highly strung horse. Most highly strung horse in the stables.' Frank bustled around the bedroom, drawing curtains, removing James's shoes, finally fetching him a glass of water from the bathroom and two painkillers.

'Now you tell me,' James muttered under his breath.

'If you took the slightest bit of interest in the horses, you would have known that it was crazy to take Monty out, especially at night and especially in bad weather. Those fields can be treacherous underfoot unless you're accustomed to it.'

James lay back with his eyes closed and wondered whether he had done any lasting damage to his body. If he never saw another horse as long as he lived, it would be too soon. And if he didn't change the conversation quickly he knew that Frank would be unstoppable, on his pet subject of why the master of the house was so uninterested in the most fascinating species of animal that had ever graced the earth. He groaned in anticipation of the sermon.

'It wasn't raining when I set off,' he mumbled.

'Overcast, though. You should have known.' Frank paused by the bed, arms folded, and shook his head.

'I would have,' James replied, 'if only I had taken up that meteorology course at university.'

'Now, now, lad, no need for sarcasm.'

Frank, in his element as he was now, made him feel like a boy. And the worst of it was that he was absolutely right. What had possessed him to go riding, incompetent rider that he was, at eight-thirty in the evening, with the threat of rain in the air?

Of course he knew. He knew, and it made him groan even louder.

'Now, time we got hold of a doctor.'

'No!' He opened his eyes, looked at Frank who was now peering worriedly at him like a mother hen, and tried to modulate his voice. 'It's just a few aches and pains. Probably bruised here and there. Nothing to worry about.' I *hate* horses, he thought. 'Nothing to call a doctor out for!'

Could he think of anything worse than Eleanor Mills trotting over here, bag in hand, to find him in this pathetic state? Thrown from a horse when he was supposed to know the damned animals like the back of his hand? It was her fault, anyway, that he'd been on the thing in the first place. Some misguided idea that he might clear her from his mind by taking a ride across the fields.

'What if something's broken?'

'I'm pretty sure I'd know about it, Frank. Broken legs tend to hurt rather more than mine does at the moment.'

'Could be a rib.'

'I'll be fine after a good night's sleep,' James said, without conviction. 'Really. Now, the best thing you can do is leave the painkillers by the bed, with some water,

and head back home.' A short walk, since Frank lived
in the grounds. He was the archetypal bachelor, whose
life and love was the stud farm. James idly wondered
whether he should sign the whole lot over to him. Nothing would make Frank happier and after this latest in-
cident there was no point in pretending that being the
owner of a string of highly bred horses did anything for
him.

'Sure you don't want the doctor?' Frank asked from
the door, and James flapped his hand in a negative gesture.

The door closed quietly, and he lay in the room with
his eyes shut and his thoughts in a mess.

There was also no point in pretending to himself any
longer that Ellie Mills was a quaint, irritating, oddly appealing doctor about whose welfare he was concerned.

The sickening truth of the matter was that, somehow,
she had wormed her way under his skin, and now she
was driving him crazy.

He had gone along to that damned nightclub with the
altruistic intention of introducing both Ellie and Henry
to the sort of life which they had probably never ex-
perienced before, what with beepers and patients and
wake-up calls and a routine that revolved around work—
and what had happened? He had ended up spending the
entire evening suffused with jealousy.

He had been enraged when she had told him that her
father liked Henry, enraged by the fact that she had taken
pains to look sexy for her fiancé, enraged by Henry's
unflappable niceness. Enraged at the thought that she
would hightail it back to London to start making wedding plans, leaving her father, the surgery and, the little
nagging voice in his head said, *him* in the lurch.

And the feeling had persisted for the balance of his
frustrating, bloody awful week.

He groaned again with a heartfelt feeling of complete

self-pity and uselessly attempted to drag up a few virtuous arguments about Eleanor Mills being far too prim and proper for someone like him. He was a red-blooded male who needed a real woman.

It's living out here, he thought to himself. It's finally getting to me. He would, he decided, hand over the reins totally to Frank and move back to London, so that he could pursue his business interests fully.

And, more to the point, he would just let Eleanor Mills get on with her life. If she wanted to abandon her duties here, then a replacement would be found, a solution arrived at. Didn't they say that necessity was the mother of invention? And if, incidentally, her marriage was an unmitigated disaster, then so be it. He would end up having the last laugh, wouldn't he?

He attempted to be philosophical about it, but visions of her rose up in his mind and relentlessly chased out every other thought.

I want her, he thought with infuriated resignation. I'm attracted to her and it doesn't matter a damn whether it's because she's a challenge, a mystery or just a curiosity that I can't seem to shake off.

The very worst of it was that he should have learnt from his wife. He was no impressionable fool, so why was he even thinking of dipping his feet into water that he knew would be boiling hot?

He covered his eyes with his hands and was beginning to drop off into sleep when there was a knock on the door.

'What?' He didn't need Frank fussing around him right now like a mother hen, bringing up cups of cocoa and a few more hard-hitting truths about his lack of interest in the horses and how he should have paid attention to his riding lessons when he was a boy.

The door opened and, silhouetted against the light from the corridor, he made out Ellie's slim figure.

'Your estate manager called me,' she said, peering into the darkness and blinking so that her eyes could adjust.

'I told him *expressly* not to get in touch with you!' James growled from the bed. He switched on the bedside light and glowered at her.

Ellie walked briskly into the room and turned on the overhead light. 'I can't see a thing with just that lamp on,' she said efficiently, and he scowled at her.

Frank would pay later for this act of high treason, he decided. He watched as she deposited her bag on the chair and then proceeded to study him thoroughly.

'There was no need for you to come out,' he muttered ungraciously. 'I suppose Frank told you what happened?'

'He said that your horse threw you.' She perched on the side of the bed and proceeded to remove the covers. 'I'm afraid you'll have to take your trousers off if I'm to examine your legs, make sure that there's nothing broken.'

'There's nothing broken.' He had imagined, in a variety of scenarios, undressing in front of her, a slow, sexual foreplay which invariably ended in bed. This was not one of those scenarios. He felt a fool.

'I think,' she said, glancing at his face, then hastily busying herself in her bag, 'that you'd better let me be the judge of that. You may have an extremely high tolerance of pain, in which case something might well be broken without your suspecting it.' Her expression, however, implied that she didn't really believe that for a minute.

She turned her back while he ponderously removed his trousers. From this vantage point, he could see the graceful curve of her neck, the way tendrils of hair curled against it, the slope of her shoulders. She had removed her jacket as she'd come in, and her thin wool cardigan was moulded provocatively against her body.

'Okay?' He lay back down on the bed and stared at the ceiling while she went to work, pressing his flesh with expert fingers, prodding. When he felt her hands on his thigh, he gritted his teeth together and tried to think distant thoughts. She had pushed up the sleeves of her cardigan so that her slender forearms were exposed. He risked a quick look downwards, noticing the outline of her breast as she examined both his legs thoroughly, then hastily resumed his inspection of the ceiling.

'How did it happen?' she asked absent-mindedly.

'Wet ground.'

'It hadn't been raining very hard, had it?'

'It also happened to be very dark,' James pointed out irritably. 'The horse was totally uncontrollable.'

'Yes. Frank did mention that you'd taken one of the more excitable horses.' She sat up. 'Nothing broken here.' She pulled the covers back over him. 'Shirt off now. I'll quickly check your ribs. It's far more likely that you might have broken one of them without realising it.'

'You mean because you assume my pain threshold is less than zero, so that if it had been a leg I would have collapsed in a faint? Needed smelling salts to revive me?' He sounded petulant, he knew, but, dammit, he felt an utter idiot. Owner of stud farm thrown by one of his own horses. Too short-sighted to know which horse to take for a canter, too moronic to realise that riding at night was a bad idea unless you happened to be a good rider. Which he wasn't.

'Did I say that?' She looked at him and raised her eyebrows expressively. Yes, the cardigan was every bit as revealing as he had suspected. Small breasts, but perfectly proportioned, and all the more arousing a sight because she was so completely unaware of her attraction.

He removed his shirt, lay back against the pillows, feeling his breathing quicken as she moved closer to him.

He imagined unbuttoning her cardigan, very slowly, and was stopped in his tracks by the thought that Henry had probably done that very thing himself. Undressed her slowly, sensuously, touched her and gazed on her wild abandon.

'I'm surprised,' she was saying, while she continued with her methodical prodding of his upper torso, 'that you were thrown. You must have quite a bit of riding experience. Did the horse get into difficulties? Was it all right?'

She was just making small talk, he realised. A doctor's habit of putting their patient at ease. Very similar to the line of chat initiated by nurses just as they were about to plunge a six-inch syringe into your arm. He wished that she would look at him and drop the doctor image. He wanted to see her blush, he wanted her to react to his proximity, even in these inauspicious circumstances. He wanted her to react to *him*, and he shook off the feeling, angry with himself.

'Well?' She wasn't looking at him.

'What?'

'The horse? Was it all right?'

'Oh, absolutely. Monty was absolutely fine. Made his way cheerfully back to the stables, in fact. He galloped right past Frank's front door, which was how he was alerted to what had happened. Oh, yes, the horse couldn't be better. Probably munching a huge meal of hay even as we speak.' He saw her mouth curve into a smile. 'As you might well suspect, I'm a fairly hopeless rider, despite my father's very patient attempts to instil some necessary skills into me at an early age.'

She was smiling openly now, that shy, hesitant way

she had of smiling, as though it wasn't something she did very often. Laughing at him, he suspected.

'You were right, nothing broken. Just a few bruises. The pain should wear off after a couple of days. In the meantime, take the usual painkillers.'

'Actually, I can cope quite well with the bruises.'

'I'm sure you can, James.' She stood up and began packing her bag and he watched her, insanely desperate to stall her now that she was getting ready to go. It was all ridiculous, he knew, but his body and his mind clearly disagreed, because he heard himself asking her to sit down.

'Well, I really need...'

'Please.' He struggled to get the word out and was only marginally heartened when she perched on the side of the bed. I have to order her to stay, he thought savagely. I have to rely on her innate politeness to sit down because I ask. What other woman had ever afforded him such a resounding compliment?

'Okay. But just for a while... I really can't stay...'

'Why do I always get the impression that you can't wait to be out of my company?' he muttered. 'Why do you always act as though you'd rather spend your time in contact with an infectious disease?'

She looked at him with a mixture of embarrassment and surprise, which made him all the more irritable. 'You're all right, you know,' she said, not quite meeting his eyes. 'It was a shock, I expect, being thrown like that...'

'I know I'm all right. And I'm not in a state of shock, so you needn't use that soothing medical voice on me. And stop,' he commanded, 'looking so nervous!'

'Was I?'

'Yes. You were. Look at the way you're sitting. As though any minute you'll take flight and leave. I don't bite, you know!'

'I would never have guessed from the way you're be-having.' She laughed. Nervously.

But, he noticed, she hadn't relaxed. Her face didn't express any nervousness, but it was there. He could see it in the way she twisted her fingers together. He could hardly *force* her to feel at ease, could he? How was it that he didn't have this sort of effect on other women? He couldn't think of a single other female who had ever treated him like this, almost like a wild animal caught in the headlights of a car. Poised to flee. He wasn't in-timidating, was he? Admittedly, he did tend towards boorishness in her presence, which brought Henry to mind—placid, restrained Henry—and that immediately sent his blood pressure up.

'Maybe you're right,' he forced himself to say. 'Maybe I'm in a state of shock. I just know that I need some company at the moment...'

'I could always call Frank and get him to come over,' she suggested, with a question in her voice.

'No, no, don't do that. Frank's had more than enough excitement for one night.' He closed his eyes and tried to adopt a relaxed pose that wouldn't alarm her. He must be desperate, he thought, if he was prepared to go to these lengths to keep a woman in a room with him for five minutes, when he knew that she'd much rather be on her way. A sick man.

'Frank's not getting any younger,' James said in a non-threatening voice.

'He's been here for a while, has he? I don't remem-ber...'

Did she have to sound so damned *polite*? 'Since I was about four. He's my right-hand man here. I only sign the cheques.'

'Well, I'll make sure that I tell him on my way out that you're okay. He was worried about you.'

'There you go again!' he snapped, opening his eyes.

'Trying to beat a retreat.' He lowered his voice to barely above a whisper. 'Is a little company too much to ask? Talk to me. Tell me about your father. How's he coming along? How are the interviews going?' In future, he decided, he would stick to the airheads. They might not have the intellectual horsepower of geniuses, but at least they didn't make him feel like this—like a pathetic fool who couldn't keep a few wayward impulses under control.

'We haven't found anyone yet,' Ellie said, eyeing him warily. 'And Father's doing fine.'

'Still going to the surgery with you?' It was a struggle to keep his eyes on her face. She wasn't, he realised, wearing a bra. He could just make out the definition of her soft nipples under the wool of her cardigan. She must have left the house in a hurry—less a personal concern than a professional response to what might have been an emergency.

'Occasionally. He's…well, actually, he's started to take an interest in cooking. He thinks that it's helping him with co-ordination with his right hand. And also he's joined a bridge circle. They meet twice a week during the day. Just retired people. He's only been a couple of times so far. I think he enjoys it.'

She was beginning to relax. He could tell from the gradual unclenching of her body. As long as the conversation did not intrude into her personal space, she would talk, but the minute she felt threatened she reacted by bringing down the shutters and putting up the exclusion zones. Why?

'And having you at home with him?'

Ellie glanced away. 'That's debatable. I suppose you could say that we're getting used to one another.'

'So in some ways the stroke has done both of you some good, anyway.' He had an insane urge to take her hand and place it very firmly on that part of him that was clamouring for her body. It would certainly snap her out of this polite question and answer routine, wouldn't it? And, by God, the thought of it alone was enough to make him tremble slightly.

'We're finding our feet. Are you feeling a bit better now? You look a little flushed.'

'Is that why you stayed?' James asked, even though he knew that it was the one question that would probably have her running for the nearest exit. 'You could at least pretend that it had something to do with wanting to chat with me for a while.' *Flushed?* Thank heavens she couldn't read what was going through his head.

Colour crept up her neck and turned her cheeks pink.

'Of course I don't mind staying here to chat with you,' she said awkwardly.

Don't mind? He wondered how he could possibly transform that admission into something resembling enthusiasm for his conversational skills. Which clearly left a lot to be desired, as far as she was concerned.

'And how's Henry?' he asked abruptly, changing the subject.

'Fine.'

The guarded look was back on her face, and he couldn't blame her. Conversations that began with him politely enquiring after Henry were destined, he knew, to degenerate into arguments. He had only recently got around to realising that jealousy had played more than its fair share in that, but of course she would never in a million years suspect that.

She was, he had discovered, on an emotional wavelength that bore little comparison to the other, well-controlled areas of her life.

'Have you given any thought to what I discussed with you?' She looked bewildered at that, and he ploughed on relentlessly. 'About staying here until things are sorted out. I don't suppose it's likely to be a vote-winner with Henry, but I personally feel that you owe it to your father to stay put until you find a suitable replacement. After all…' he knew that he shouldn't say it, but he went ahead anyway '…you've spent enough of your past avoiding your life here…'

'I hope you're not trying to use emotional blackmail on me,' Ellie said angrily, leaning forward and affording him an almost irresistible view of her cleavage—just visible. He almost groaned.

'I'm trying to get you to evaluate where your priorities lie.'

'And what business is it of yours?'

'Has it ever occurred to you that you've spent most of your life running away, and that if you return to London now and leave your father in the lurch you'll just be continuing the trend?'

'I have *not* run away! From anything!' But he could tell from her high colour and the tremor in her voice that he had struck a nerve. Oh, to reach in and pull out intimacies from her!

'Your home life was less than ideal, so you ran away. You hid in your books, then in your silences with your father, then in your career. You had a bad affair with a man when you were young, so what did you do? You ran into great, protective Henry. When do you stop running, Ellie? When do you confront your problems and try to sort them out?'

'You don't know a thing about me!' Her voice was unsteady, but she was focusing on him now, hearing every word he was saying, taking it all in.

'Does anyone? Do you trust anyone with your life?'

'Do you care, James Kellern? Don't think that I don't know what you're doing—trying to goad me into a response. The only thing on your mind is whether I stay here or not. You think I'm selfish, I know that. Selfish for not coming up to visit Father once a month, selfish for forging a career for myself when I should be at home having babies and looking after a husband.'

James looked at her and quite honestly didn't know what he thought. He thought that she was like fire, like a soft breeze blowing through a glade, like the sea at night, like every force of nature that couldn't be pinned down.

'When do you intend to go back to London?' he asked abruptly.

'I'm not sure. Next week some time... There are three patients I want to see, then I'll be back. You needn't worry that this engagement ring is going to pull me back to London before I find a replacement for the surgery.'

'I'm glad to hear it.' At the mention of that damned engagement ring, he felt like dragging it off her finger and chucking it in the bin. Running and hiding. That was what she was doing, and had been doing for all her life. If he could see that, then why on earth couldn't she? It escaped him how he could be even remotely attracted to a woman whom he spent half his time wanting to shake.

'Good. Now I really think it's time I left.' She stood up and he reached out, a reflex action, and pulled her back down to the bed, holding onto her wrist, partly to keep her where she was, partly because he liked the feel of her skin beneath his fingers.

'What do you think you're doing?' She tried to pull free, but he wasn't about to let her run away—though what he hoped to achieve with this little display of masculine force was beyond him. Apart from alienating her even further. What the hell was happening to him?

'Let me go!'

'No.'

'What?'

'I said, no. I'm not going to let you go, because there's something else I want to talk to you about.' He at-

tempted a reassuring smile, but she looked far from re-
assured. In fact, she looked positively alarmed.

Yet he couldn't let her walk away, and he didn't
understand why. What game was this he was playing?
One he had never played before, and there seemed to be
no rules. He had never had to forcibly manacle a woman
just to get her to talk to him, had never wanted to—yet
here he was, acting so out of character that he could
hardly recognise himself. Was it any wonder that she
was staring at him as though he were deranged?

'What?' He could feel her light perspiration under his
fingers.

'Last Saturday…' he began, hitting on the subject
quite randomly because it was the only thing that came
to mind.

'What about last Saturday?'

'I have to confess that I arranged to take you both to
that nightclub on purpose.'

'*You* arranged?'

'Your father called purely for a chat, and in the course
of the conversation he mentioned that Henry was down
for the weekend. So I suggested to him that it might be
an idea for Henry to see something of our lovely city
rather than stay cooped up in the house for the entire
time.'

'And how exactly did you do that?' Ellie asked,
astounded.

'I may have mentioned, in passing, that Henry might
find four walls and the countryside a little claustrophobic, when he was probably used to rather more excitement in London…'

It had seemed a damned clever idea at the time, and
he had felt self-righteously altruistic when he had arranged it. There was no point in stepping into one life
if you had no other by way of comparison, was there?
Why go from a steady, unexciting non-marital state into

a steady, unexciting marital state without at least first sampling what else there was on offer? At least, that was how he had viewed the situation at the time. It had only dawned on him afterwards that his motives might not have been quite as high-minded as he'd pretended to himself.

Ellie was staring at him now, open-mouthed. 'But you'd met Henry,' she said in a ragged voice. 'You gave me a long lecture on his unsuitability on the grounds that he wasn't exciting enough! Henry's a homebody at heart, so why on earth would you pretend otherwise?'

James wished he hadn't mentioned anything in the first place. He wished he'd kept his mouth shut. Wasn't there some myth about the messenger being slaughtered because the message was bad news?

However, now that he had embarked on his narrative, he couldn't spot a way out. 'He's a homebody because he's probably had no experience of anything else.'

'So you decided that you'd show him another side of life, is that it? A great, charitable act, courtesy of James Kellern! And I suppose you arranged for that tall, dark-haired girl to aid and abet?'

'Don't be ridiculous.'

'Then what?' Her eyes flared angrily. 'Stay out of my life! Stop trying to interfere in things that don't concern you!'

'Has Henry been the same since...?' The question was a gamble, but the answer was there in that flicker of hesitation in her eyes. He felt a rush of elation, tinged with only the slightest sheepishness at the underhandedness of his ruse. 'He hasn't, has he...?'

Ellie ignored the question, but her cheeks were flaming. 'Do I tell you how to conduct your life? I don't give you long lectures on the unsuitability of women who are only useful to you as bed partners, and I'll bet my job that no one else does either! No one would dare! Don't you think that I'm intelligent enough to know what I'm doing?'

'You're incredibly intelligent and I have no doubt that you know precisely what you're doing—when it comes to your work. But you're as naive as hell in other respects.' God, did she have any idea how beautiful she looked when she was angry like that? With her cheeks red and her eyes glittering like jewels? He felt as though he was operating in a completely different stratosphere, where the air was different and everything around him was heightened to breaking point.

'Oh, and you know, do you? You know so much about the human psyche that you couldn't even hold your own marriage together!' She looked at him, distraught, but he was not in the least offended by what she had said—although if anyone else had dared say as much he would have lashed out instinctively, shielding his private affairs from public eyes.

'You're absolutely right. On paper, Antonia and I were eminently suited for marriage. Both intelligent, both high achievers, both invigorated by the demands of work. In fact, both operating on perfectly parallel lines— but parallel lines in marriage don't work, do they? On a deeper level, we were wildly unsuitable, which is why the marriage eventually fell apart at the seams.'

He searched her face, wondering whether he should drag Henry back into the conversation. He didn't know why, but the marriage thing seemed to have taken hold of him. Now he felt a crusading zeal to put the dampeners on what he foresaw as certain failure. He had to make her understand.

'Look at the pair of you, Ellie,' he said urgently. 'On paper, you and Henry are eminently suitable and I have no doubt that he's a very comfortable person for you to be with, but what price do you put on comfort and safety?' His grip slackened on her wrist, but he still didn't let go, even though he knew that she wouldn't run away now. She might not have wanted to sit here and listen to him in the first place, but he could see that she was too absorbed in what he was saying to make her escape, even though it was a situation she had not courted.

'What's wrong with wanting to be safe?' she whispered. 'I grew up hardly knowing my father. I had independence and self-reliance forced on me. Is it a crime to aspire to a little comfort?'

James wanted to shake her. Instead, he took a deep breath and continued, less urgently but no less emphatically, 'Safety can end up being the bars of a cage. It can end up suffocating the natural impulse to strive for happiness.'

'I don't want to hear this.' She tore her hand away from his and covered her ears, a childish gesture that he found profoundly touching.

'The point I'm making is that I really don't think that Henry's lived at all. Think back to how he was at the nightclub. He acted as though his entire life had been devoted to matters of grave concern, and for the first time he'd been allowed to let his hair down and just have a good time.'

Ellie's hands dropped to her sides. 'I don't stand in the way of Henry having a good time. It's not my fault that my life is more ruled by work than his is. We're both doctors, but my area of practice just happens to require more hours.'

'And what about you, Ellie? Have *you* lived? Or have you dedicated your whole life to becoming a doctor?' It was like talking to a brick wall, he thought with frustration. It was all so clear to him—how could she fail to see things in the same light as he did? She wanted to go through life without any ripples appearing to disturb the placid predictability of things, but life just wasn't like that. It was the ripples that gave life its edge.

'That's not fair!' Ellie exclaimed, and he had to tear his mind back to what he had been saying.

'No, I don't suppose it is, but all I'm asking is for you to look honestly at yourself and at what you want out of life. It's one thing working things out in your head, but the decisions you reach with your head never come to anything unless your heart follows suit. Can you honestly say that this marriage is a good idea?'

He realised, with a little consternation, that he sounded sanctimonious. Had he ever sounded sanctimonious in his life before? Not that he could remember. In fact, he couldn't remember ever preaching to anyone about their decisions in life. He had always believed that adults were entitled to get on with their own mistakes and that, anyway, advice dispensed was rarely followed.

'I think you've spent your life so wrapped up in your pursuit of a medical career that there's a whole chunk of living that's bypassed you.' He groaned inwardly at this preposterous display of home-grown wisdom. He also had the feeling that he was losing the reins of the conversation. He couldn't take his eyes away from her face.

'In other words, you think I'm boring,' he heard her say, without really analysing *what* she was saying. 'You've never come right out and said so, but I'm not blind. You think that I'm a power-hungry woman with a limited social life and an inability to do anything apart from my job. Why don't you come right out and say it? Why beat about the bush with lots of questions and innuendoes?'

What was she saying? The words flowed over his head. He followed the movement of her lips with the intensity of a man trying to lip-read.

'You have a wonderful mouth,' he murmured huskily.

'What?' Ellie looked at him and he could read sudden, wild confusion in her eyes.

'Your mouth. It's a very vulnerable mouth.' He leaned across and, amazed to find that he felt as nervous as a fifteen-year-old boy, put his hand behind her head and drew her towards him.

There was panic in her as she tried to pull away, but something else too. Some other force, beating inside her, mirrored in her eyes. He recognised in her the same dangerous pull of desire as he was feeling. She moaned a denial, but her eyes, when they met his, were feverish, burning with the same need. Fear. That was it. He could sense it. She was afraid of what she was feeling.

'There's nothing to be afraid of.' His voice seemed to come from a long way away, and he didn't hear her response, if indeed she made one, because suddenly the need to touch her was so overpowering that he held her head with both his hands and brought her mouth to his.

His lips moved over hers and he thrust his tongue inside her mouth, a deep, hungry exploration. He more than half expected her to push him away, but she didn't, and the unexpectedness of her acquiescence turned him on in a way he would never have imagined possible.

She closed her eyes and leaned back and he kissed her neck, light, delicate, sensuous kisses, tasting her skin under his tongue and aroused by the raggedness of her breathing.

'You mustn't,' she whispered, groaning. 'You don't know what you're doing. Neither of us does!'

'I know.' His voice was low and unsteady and he couldn't stop kissing her. He was helpless with need. For once, he was no longer master of his impulses. Somewhere along the way, they had taken over. Had he ever felt desire like this before?

He traced the contours of her ear with his tongue and she expelled a trembling sigh of pleasure.

'Please, James...we mustn't...' He could hear that fear again, but overlying it was the pull of desire, the breathless, bewildered sound of physical attraction. He could sense both tearing through her and he kissed her harder, not wanting to lose her to logic.

He murmured something incoherent and pulled her against him, groaning when she moved against his body with the feline sleekness of a cat stretching against its owner's legs.

'Do you want me to stop? Tell me now.' Could he muster up some self-control from somewhere? He tried to remind himself that passion was just a burning flame that could be extinguished. He touched her thigh and found he could hardly breathe.

'No, don't stop.' She trembled. 'I want you.'

CHAPTER SEVEN

THERE, it was out. The shameful truth which she had been hiding, uselessly, from herself. The admission made her feel naked, stripped for the first time in her life of all her defences. Hadn't this been what she had feared most? The knowledge that this man, appearing like a dark shadow, could alter all the confines of her life?

Ellie looked at him, then looked away. Inside, it was as though a thousand birds had taken flight. She could feel the beating of their wings against her chest, she could feel the weakness of need struggling against common sense.

'I'll switch the light off,' James said huskily, and she hurriedly stood up.

'No. I mean, I'll do it. I'll switch it off.' She couldn't wait to have a bit of darkness around her, something to help conceal her nervousness at what was happening, and what was about to happen. She felt completely out of control, but what was the point of trying to re-establish her composure? What was the point of trying to fight this hold he had over her?

He would never force her to sleep with him; she knew that. But running away would get her nowhere, because she would still have all those confusing, powerful urges inside her and it would be only a matter of time before she found herself back in the same situation. He had been right when he had told her that she had spent her life running. Sooner or later, her legs would just simply give out.

She sat on the bed next to him, torn between agony and anticipation.

'Tell me you haven't changed your mind.' James's voice was casual but his eyes were intent.

'James…it's not right…I'm engaged…' The engagement had seemed so right at the time. Now, with hindsight, she could see it for what it really was: a desperate attempt to get her life in order. She tried to think of Henry, but she could hardly hold his image in her head for more than a few seconds. This man next to her was too consuming—he blocked out everything and everyone.

'The engagement was a mistake; why don't you admit it? You can't hide behind Henry, hope that he takes care of your emotional needs.'

'It's all right for you!'

'Why?'

'This is madness,' she whispered. Now she was looking at him, drinking him in. Yes, it was madness, a madness that turned sanity into a joke. She badly wanted to touch him, but she felt that if she did her hand might go up in flames.

'Why? Why is it madness? Because it's never happened to you before? Because it isn't sanitised and degermed like one of your medical instruments?'

'Because…' Her breathing came thick and fast and she half closed her eyes in an attempt to get a grip on herself. Why was it madness? She couldn't follow the thought through, yet she just knew that it was.

He reached out to place his hand behind her head and pulled her towards him, so that he could lick the side of her mouth with his tongue.

'Undress me,' he murmured into her ear. His voice was thick, unsteady, but held the power of command—or maybe her hands were simply obeying their own dictates.

Thank God the light had been switched off. She was trembling as she undid his trousers. Her hands brushed his bare skin in the process and she had a fleeting sensation of sudden heat, as though she had been branded.

'Don't look away,' he groaned as she eased off his boxer shorts. 'I want you to see what you do to me.'

So she risked a look, and a shudder of excitement raced through her at the sight of his erection. And now she found that she couldn't tear her eyes away from his body. It was as though she had never seen a naked man in her life before, but perhaps his impact on her was stronger because he was so incredibly beautiful to look at. Lean, muscular, at ease with his nakedness.

She began unbuttoning her cardigan, and he stopped her.

'Stand up to undress. Let me see you. Take your time. I want this moment in time to last for ever.' His voice was rough, and for a moment Ellie hesitated, not quite knowing what to do. She wasn't accustomed to turning the simple act of disrobing into a performance, and she could feel all her years of inbred primness rushing up inside her. Then he said huskily, 'Go on. I want to lie here and drink you in. Two mad people in a mad world.'

Ellie stood up and self-consciously undid the buttons of her cardigan. She wasn't ashamed of her body. As bodies went, she thought that hers was in pretty good form considering that she was in her thirties. On the other hand, she was fully aware that she was no nubile teenager. She was also aware of the fact that he was a connoisseur of female bodies, and she agonisingly concluded that hers would not head the list.

She glanced shyly at him, searching for any sign of possible disgust on his face, but he was smiling, his eyes roving hotly over her, and she felt an unaccustomed thrill of power. Strange, but everything seemed to be happening on a different plane—a dangerous, beguiling plane, some place she'd never been before.

She removed the cardigan with more confidence. When he saw her breasts, she heard him gasp with desire.

'I'm not exactly a spring chicken any more,' she whispered, moving towards the bed, naked.

'You're the best thing I've ever seen,' James said, wrapping his arms around her as she slipped in next to him. He kissed her earlobe, nipping it gently with his teeth, then her neck, and her body arched back to receive the lingering caresses.

'I've wanted you…it seems in a way that I've never wanted a woman in my life before.' He stroked her thigh with his hand while he spoke, a slow, steady movement. The glitter of his eyes mesmerised her but down below her body was responding in a far more frantic manner to his fingers, which were now touching her lightly, then exploring the soft, wet core that opened to his fingers like a flower.

She moved gainst him, trembling, arching upwards. He lowered his head to her breasts, flicking his tongue over the hardened nipples, then covering them, first one, then the other, with his mouth until he was sucking the erect tips, drawing them into his mouth and sending a million wild, electric currents through her body.

Had she ever made love before? It seemed not. Not like this, at any rate. Her body was alive, pulsating under the combined touch of his mouth and his fingers.

When his mouth left her breasts to continue a downward exploration, she continued massaging them herself, playing with her nipples, rolling them between her fingers. She was no longer Eleanor Mills. She was some wild, abandoned creature, one she could hardly recognise.

He parted her legs with his hands, and she felt his

tongue replace his fingers, probing inside her, and she squirmed against it. She was slippery with desire and his tongue, finding her throbbing, engorged nub of pleasure, sucked and wriggled until she felt dizzy with a need to reach fulfilment.

Her body, when he finally thrust into her, was ready for his, already at a peak of excitement, and their rhythmic movements were fast and abandoned. A hot, furious surge of passion and fulfilment.

It was only afterwards that the reality of what they had done hit home and she turned to him.

'So…' she murmured.

'So…' His voice echoed hers and he stroked the side of her face with his fingers, which made her shiver.

She placed her hand on his chest and looked at her fingers, spread flat. 'Actually, I'm wondering what happens next,' she said in a rush. 'I mean…' What did she mean? She could feel confusion threading its way through her thoughts again, like a treacherous worm that wouldn't allow her any self-control.

'I think you ought to break off your engagement with Henry.' His body went still as he waited for her answer. 'Don't you?'

'Yes, I suppose so.'

'Just *suppose*?' He laughed under his breath, but there was a certain tightness in his voice.

'I just feel so guilty about… I'm afraid I rushed in without giving it any thought at all. That's not like me. Normally, I always stop to think…'

'Always?'

'It's my nature.' She was beginning, though, to wonder exactly what her nature was. Ever since she had met James Kellern, she had acted out of character. She was a grown woman. Surely her personality could not be so unformed that one man could have had such an effect on it? Or perhaps, she thought, allowing herself the benefit of the doubt, it had been the irregularity of the situation that had caused it. She had never had to cope with any illness in her father before, had never had to go beyond the parameters of their rigid relationship. Everything, recently, had seemed new. James, quite possibly, was just one peripheral element in all of this. The thought gave her a moment's comfort, because it made her feel less vulnerable.

'Natures change,' he told her.

'Do they?' She lay back and had the strangest feeling: scared, yet powerful enough to climb a thousand mountains.

'They do.' He stroked her stomach, then the swell of her thigh. 'It's true what they say about expecting the unexpected. Life's full of sudden turnings. I don't suppose you ever stopped to consider that anything might happen to change the course of your neatly plotted life...'

'You make me sound very dull...'

'Can you deny that there was a certain element of predictability to your life?'

'No. Not when you put it like that.' Every day had been different, it was true. Every emergency had required different responses, but overall her days had been predictable, full of situations which were variations on a theme, and her life outside work had been equally predictable. Meals out with Henry, friends whom she saw as often as she could, which amounted to only very occasionally. Emotionally, she had had everything sewn up, with nothing surprising to alter the tenor of her life.

Now things seemed to have changed and it was as if solid ground had given way to quicksand.

'Things were comfortable the way they were,' she said defensively.

'Henry is a comfortable kind of chap,' James told her, pausing in his caress. 'Too comfortable for you.'

Which, she thought confusedly, isn't to say that you, as the opposite extreme, are any more suited to me than he is.

But he was right in that she should never have allowed herself to get swept up in an engagement to a man in the manner of someone drifting on a tide. She hadn't really contemplated the other alternative, which was to head against the current in the opposite direction, whatever the perils there might be. Running away.

'I don't want to talk about this any more,' she said brokenly, reaching up to run shaking fingers through his hair, and he caught her wrist in a loose grip.

'Because I'm asking you questions that you can't answer?'

'Do you ever stop being bossy?' She laughed and there was a catch behind the laughter. Yes, she wanted to say, because I have no answers, and for a thousand other reasons you disturb me. But I can't stop this crazy yearning.

He relaxed and nuzzled against her neck and the light, tickling kisses made her tremble again as desire reawakened inside her.

He cupped the weight of her breast, caressing it with his hand while his thumb stroked her nipple into erect hardness, and she moaned and closed her eyes. It was blessed relief to let pure sensation take over from confusing thought. It vaguely crossed her mind that she ought to telephone her father, let him know where she was without mentioning what precisely was going on, but the intention was soon lost under James's exploration of her body. How could she reasonably be expected to do something as ordinary as make a phone call when her body was aflame and her mind had wondrously shut down?

It was only much later, hours later in fact, when she was standing at the front door, back in her now slightly creased clothes and feeling very dishevelled even though her reflection had earlier assured her that she looked perfectly all right, that she formulated the question which had more or less been on her mind since she had entered his bedroom.

'Where do we go from here?' Her voice managed to attain just the right note of casualness which she felt was needed. He wasn't the sort of man who appreciated being forced into a corner. She had heard enough, firsthand, of his unwillingness to commit to a relationship in the wake of his disastrous marriage.

And anyway she was not ready for any kind of relationship with him beyond the transient, was she? Henry, she realised now, had been a great error of judgement, a reaction to an assortment of circumstances, a wish to flee back to what she knew rather than confront what she didn't. She wasn't about to allow any other emotion to take her down the road of poor judgement.

'You tell Henry that the engagement is off...'

'I think we've already covered that ground.'

'And who knows?' He stuck his hands in the pockets of his trousers, which he had put on hastily and left unbuttoned at the waist. 'How do you feel about seeing me on a fairly regular basis while you're here?'

That sounded about as casual as she assumed she wanted, but she still found herself having to stifle a swift, overpowering feeling of disappointment.

'I'm not looking for involvement,' Ellie told him, working on the premise that it was better to lay down the rules which would leave her free to hold onto her pride when their brief acquaintanceship came to an end. 'I don't intend making the same mistake that I did with Henry.'

'Which was?' His voice was curiously lacking in inflection.

'Which was encouraging a relationship that really had

no chance of permanent success.' She frowned, wondering whether she sounded as though she was turning down a proposal for intimacy which hadn't even been offered. He had freely admitted on more than one occasion that she was not his type of woman. Logical deduction meant that he saw her as an interesting but passing affair, someone who had aroused his curiosity but little more.

'In other words, no strings attached.'

'In other words…' she agreed, not meeting his eyes.

'What,' he asked, 'are you doing tomorrow night?' He sounded normal once again. His normality helped.

'Nothing planned.'

'I'll pick you up at seven-thirty. We could have a meal and then go to the theatre afterwards.'

'Could we make it the cinema instead?' she asked, and he raised his eyebrows with barely disguised curiosity. 'I'm a bit of a sucker for movies,' she said, feeling as though she was confessing to an illicit, secret sin. 'I know that going to the theatre is a more…a more cultured experience—probably more rewarding as well. But movies help me to relax.'

'Any type of movie in particular, or just all movies in general?' He tucked her hair behind her ear, which seemed to her a very sweet, tender thing to do, and then stuck his hand back into his pocket.

'All movies in general,' Ellie said, laughing a little self-consciously because that small gesture had disoriented her. 'But I rather enjoy funny ones. Funny ones with happy endings.'

'Funny ones with happy endings. I'll see what I can do.'

He didn't kiss her, but smiled instead, a warm, amused smile that made her feel foolishly happy. Made her feel, in fact, like a kid of sixteen. When, she asked herself, was the last time she had felt like that? Had she *ever* felt like that?

She didn't want to analyse the feeling too much, just in case it disappeared, but for the rest of the night and the whole of the following day she continued to walk on air. Now and then, a shadow would disturb the horizon, but it wasn't difficult chasing those shadows away. What was she doing except opening herself up to a freedom she had never tasted before? She had fought her war, battled against the impulse, so what if she had now given in?

Still, she made an effort to be subdued when she telephoned Henry early that evening, while her father was having supper.

She listened with nervous impatience while he went through the usual formal, polite preliminaries, asking her how she was, what she'd been up to, then volunteering information on what he'd been doing. As soon as there was a decent break in the conversation, she said, hesitantly, that there was something she had to say to him.

Funny, she thought, how bad news always seemed to come wrapped up in the same packaging. A tone of voice, a certain silence.

'What?' Henry asked, with equal hesitation. She could imagine him frowning, speculating on what she could be about to say.

'I've been thinking,' Ellie said, and she twisted the curly telephone cord around her fingers and released it suddenly, watching it reform into its original shape. 'I've been thinking about us, Henry,' she ploughed on, when silence greeted her observation.

'Oh, yes.'

'Henry, I'm not sure how to say this—'

'I've been thinking too,' he interrupted her. 'Perhaps we rushed into this engagement. Or maybe I should say that perhaps I rushed you into this engagement.'

Ellie realised that she was wearing a dumbfounded expression on her face.

'I was going to call you,' she heard him say down the line, and she frantically tried to identify the expression on his face from the tone of his voice. 'The thing is, Ellie, we both need a little space, I think. Perhaps it would be a good idea if we called it off, at least temporarily. Of course, you'll still be my greatest friend, but...'

Relief rushed to her head, making her feel dizzy and suddenly tender towards him.

'And likewise, Henry. I'm really sorry. I guess we both kind of...'

'Drifted into it.'

Ellie digested this. 'When did you first...first realise this?' she asked. He had seemed as attentive as usual when he had come over for the weekend, and the sudden, virtually overnight change had taken her by surprise. Henry had always been such a predictable person, yet here he was, behaving in a manner that showed how little she had known him. Maybe, she thought, people rarely knew very much about the other people in their lives, however close they were. You meandered along in relationships, thinking that you knew everything you could possibly know about someone, but perhaps, at the end of the day, all you really knew was what they wanted you to.

Or maybe, she mused, she just hadn't had the right key to open Henry up.

He was talking to her about the nightclub in Dublin, telling her that for the first time he had seen a part of life that he had previously missed.

'The part,' he admitted sheepishly, 'that most people go through when they're at university, or before. Except that...'

'You were too wrapped up in studying...? Me too,'

Ellie said, with a little laugh. Had they never talked about this before? They must have, but she couldn't remember.

Would they now be able to make something of their relationship? she wondered. Now that this was out in the open? No. She didn't hold the key to Henry, and he didn't hold the key to her. But at least they would part company as friends, which was what she had hoped.

The call over, she broke the news to her father. She didn't know what she expected his response to be and for once she did not anticipate the worst.

'I made a mistake, Father,' she said bravely.

'We all do, at some point.' He looked at her and said heavily, 'Was that why you asked me about your mother? About whether we felt right about getting married?'

Ellie threw him a cautious, surprised glance. 'I... Yes...' She paused. 'I suppose you think I'm fickle,' she said, plunging onwards clumsily.

'Sensible.' He looked at her shrewdly. 'Better now than later.'

'I don't normally make such a mess of things, Father.'

'Does one good, now and then, to make a mess of things.'

If she looked down she would fall. That was how she felt. Little steps, here and there, but now she could see the distance she and her father had covered over the past few weeks. A year ago she would not have dreamed of letting her father see her emotions, but things had changed. Or maybe she had never had any emotions for him to see, before. No, she had. Whether she wanted to admit the truth behind what James had said or not, she *had* hidden herself away. Now she would enter into dialogue whether her father wanted to or not. She would stop bottling things up and pretending that what she hid from herself was not really there.

'Have you ever made a mess of anything, Father?'
She looked at him and he went red. In fact, he remained
silent for so long that she was on the point of apologising
for the question, when he said guiltily, 'Well, I didn't
do all I could for you, did I?'

'Did you blame me for for Mother's death?'

'Whatever gave you that idea?' He looked horrified—
so horrified that she was ashamed to admit that the
thought had plagued her from as far back as she could
remember.

'I know you wanted a son…'

'I was grateful for the daughter I got.' He would never
apologise, she knew, for any mistakes he had made with
her. But it was enough that he could come this close to
admitting them, enough that she could begin to see
through the opaque curtain that had shrouded their relationship.

She suddenly thought how far away London seemed.
A lifetime away. She had been a different person then.
She might not know who she was now, but she was
discovering—and it was a journey she would make if it
killed her in the process.

In the restaurant that night, sitting opposite James, she
allowed her foolish heart to do any number of pole
vaults, and for the first time she made no attempt to
rationalise it back into conformity.

'You're wearing a dreamy expression…' he said at
one point, and Ellie smiled at him and blamed it on the
alcohol. But alcohol had nothing to do with it. Her mind
was free and so was her body—or at least heading in
that direction?

'Happy?' he murmured later, as they were leaving the
restaurant, and she slipped her arm through his.

'Father and I are actually beginning to talk to one
another,' Ellie heard herself say.

'And you're utterly surprised.'

'Would it go to your head if I told you that you were right when you said that I had to stop running away from the situation?'

'It might, but carry on anyway.'

As they drove to the cinema, Ellie talked as though a dam had been released.

'I think I stopped giving Father a chance when I was a child. I was too young to understand that he wasn't rejecting me, he was simply recovering from Mother's death and then doing his best to bring up a child single-handedly.'

'And now that you've got that straight it's all plain sailing?'

'Well, not quite yet, but I'm determined to come over and see him more often. Much more often. Get him over to London. It's late, but it's not too late to try and construct a few bridges.'

'Sure you won't get there and find that you just can't fit him into your schedule after all?'

'What is that supposed to mean?'

'That you're back to square one, back to fitting things around your schedule in London.'

She could only see his profile, but she could tell he was glaring. How was it that she still only seemed to notice the sensuous lines of his face, the way his eyelashes fanned his cheeks when he looked down? Was it the wine? Or was it that she just felt too mellow to rise to an argument?

'Oh, come on, James,' she said coaxingly. 'Stop glaring. It doesn't suit you. You'll end up with terrible frown lines.'

To her surprise, he smiled slowly. 'You're so damned bossy, Eleanor Mills.'

'Thanks very much!' She smiled back and concentrated on the scenery. Lazy evening traffic, people going out to have a bit of fun. In London, she rarely noticed things like this. Life was so quick, frenetic really. She could talk about going back there, picking up the pieces from where she had left them, but the reality would be quite different.

And what about James? Her mind refused to indulge in the reality of that, the reality of London, of not seeing him again, of relegating this relationship to the past. It might well not belong to the future, but she could not seem to think of it in terms of the past either.

What was going to happen when a replacement was found and her time in Ireland was up?

She hadn't realised, until now, how embedded she had become in being a rural practitioner. She hadn't realised, until now, how much there was to appreciate in a slower lifestyle.

She closed her mind to unsettling thoughts, and was smiling by the time they reached the cinema.

In the darkness of the auditorium, watching what was turning out to be a dull movie involving a complicated espionage plot with quite a bit of gratuitous violence and a cast of actors and actresses who seemed permanently bewildered by whatever was going on, the only person she could think of was James. She could feel him next to her, a dark presence.

When she leaned over to ask him something, he didn't answer. Instead, he cupped her face with his hand and asked her whether she was enjoying the movie.

'I might enjoy it more if I knew what exactly was going on,' Ellie told him, hearing a catch in her voice.

'I understand perfectly what's going on,' he informed her, 'but I could think of something else that I'd enjoy rather more.'

'What?'

'You.' He kissed her with lingering thoroughness. 'I've been wanting to do that all evening,' he murmured into her ear, and his warm breath sent a shiver through her.

The words, the tone of his voice made her shudder. She was certain that if he told her to unbutton her dress so that he could touch her she would willingly do so. She who had never been at the beck and call of anyone, and who had cultivated her independence like a talisman against vulnerability.

He didn't ask her to unbutton anything. Instead, they made a stealthy exit from the cinema, like two teenagers, slipped into his car and headed out of the city and towards his house.

Surrounded by the velvety night, as the city lights dimmed behind them, devoured gradually by sprawling countryside, he ran his hand along her thigh, higher and higher until he bypassed her thin stockings and felt her flesh.

Ellie slipped a little lower in her seat, breathing quickly, her eyes half-closed. He was driving slowly now, with only one hand on the wheel. His eyes were on the road, and his other hand was on her thigh, and then inside her lacy underwear, so that he could feel her moist response.

She moaned and heard him say thickly, 'This is no good. I have to stop.' And the car was no longer moving. They were in a dark lay-by at the side of the road and she felt a sharp thrill of excitement as she contemplated doing something that so many teenagers had done before, but which was something she had never done herself.

CHAPTER EIGHT

LATER—much later, it seemed—they drove slowly back to James's house.

He felt like whistling, or else bursting into song. In the darkness of the car, he stole sidelong glances at Ellie, but her profile was averted as she stared out of the window and he couldn't read the expression on her face. God, he felt *alive*. Amazing. He couldn't remember ever having felt this way after making love to a woman. Replete, yes. Satisfied, definitely. But never like this—filled with a wild, restless energy that made him feel as though he could keep going all night, all year, without pausing to let reality in. He grinned to himself and drummed his fingers on the steering wheel.

'What are you thinking?' he asked eventually, curious to know what was going through Ellie's head. He wished that he could read her every thought, turn her every emotion inside out, have complete and total access to her mind. He glanced swiftly at her.

'Not much. Just finding it hard to believe that we just did…what we did…'

Her words made him feel strangely gratified. Her face, in the shadows of the car, was soft. As was her voice. Was this why he found her so absurdly alluring? he wondered. Because he was allowed a glimpse of the vulnerable girl behind the hard-edged, competent exterior? He had never thought that there was much mystery involved in relationships with women. Now he just wasn't certain.

'Sex,' he said with a smile, 'is a perfectly natural occurrence between consenting adults who are mutually attracted.'

'You sound like a handbook.'

James laughed and threw her an appreciative look. He liked that dry, understated sense of humour. Most of the women he had dated in the past enjoyed the slip-on-a-banana-skin category of humour, whilst Antonia, he had realised during the course of their marriage, had none at all.

'Don't tell me that you've never made love in the back seat of a car,' he teased, still smiling. When she answered, however, there wasn't the same amusement in her voice. She sounded thoughtful.

'Is that so unusual?'

'Not highly,' he said, and then, because he couldn't resist it, he added, 'Although I might have thought that you and Henry... Didn't you ever...?'

'Neither of us owns a car in London,' she said. 'So that would have been a little on the difficult side to achieve.'

He wished that he hadn't brought Henry up in the conversation. The good feeling was evaporating and he could sense the onset of a very grim mood. Henry was history, he consoled himself. A mistake that had been rectified before it was too late. Still, mistake or no mistake, she must have felt *something* for him, and possibly the mere mention of his name had brought back a host of unwelcome memories. He could have kicked himself.

'What's the matter?' he asked.

'Nothing.'

'Usually when a woman says ''Nothing'' in that tone of voice she means ''Something, but I'm not ready to divulge it yet''.'

'Oh, and you should know, James. After all the experience you've had with the opposite sex.'

They pulled up in the courtyard of the house and as soon as they were inside he turned to her and said abruptly, 'Look, why don't you just spit it out?'

'Could I at least remove my coat first?' She looked up at him, her fair hair swept over one shoulder. Even though her expression was serious, he still felt an incredible urge to kiss her, to pull her towards him, to feel the curve of her slender body against his.

Not a good idea, that. She would rightly accuse him of being preoccupied with sex. Damn stupid thing was, she'd never understand that it wasn't so much a preoccupation with sex as a complete inability even to set eyes on her without wanting to touch her.

He hung her coat up and offered her a drink. She replied that a cup of coffee would be nice, so they made their way into the kitchen and he obligingly made them both some coffee, making sure not to look at her too hard or for too long, just in case he found himself giving in to the need to touch her.

'Right.' He sat down facing her. 'Talk to me.'

'Someone has applied for the vacancy.'

'Oh, yes?' He hadn't expected this. It was an interesting development, he told himself. Interesting and inevitable, and he forced himself to look suitably intrigued. 'And when did all this happen?'

'Today, actually.' Her eyes swooped down and she blushed. 'I forgot all about it or else I would have mentioned it to you at the restaurant.'

'You forgot?' How, he wanted to demand, could you forget something that has the potential to wreck what we've got going? Then he remembered that this was little more than a passing relationship for both of them and he injected some civilised interest into his voice. 'So tell me about him.' Did she have to look so damned *remote*? he thought irritably.

'He's a young chap. Derek Clayton.' She looked at him with animation, which he found almost as irritating as the remote expression. In fact, he thought sourly, she looked positively thrilled at the development. 'The unusual thing about him is that he's not our average thwarted surgeon, settling on general practice as second best. He genuinely wanted to be a GP and the bonus is that he was born and raised in a small village on the coast so he knows what it's like living in a small community. More to the point, he enjoys that kind of lifestyle. He has a young wife and they hope to start a family soon, and he thinks that this is just the right place to bring up children.'

'Really?' He could barely get the word out.

'Yes, really.' She smiled at him and he bared his teeth politely in response.

'And what does your father make of him?'

'They seemed to get along rather well. Derek's assured him that he will find Father's input invaluable, for as long as he wants to be a part of the surgery. But to be honest Father doesn't seem quite so bothered as he was when I first arrived. I think he'd spent so much time living for his work that he never realised how much else there was out there. He'd be more than happy just to do the odd spot of pottering now and again. I mean, he's got his bridge circle, and he's recently joined an operatic club for pensioners, which I gather means lots of heavily subsidised trips around the country to opera houses. He's even expressed an interest in taking up painting as a hobby.'

'In other words, he no longer gives a damn who replaces you when you leave, just so long as they're not patently incompetent or boorishly unbearable to get along with.' He knew how he sounded. It definitely wasn't adult, civilised and concerned and he hated himself for it.

'Of course he gives a damn! Anyway, Derek Clayton seems perfect for the job. Young enough to be enthusiastic and not daunted by the prospect of living in such a small place. Why aren't you giving me any support?'

'Why the hell do you think?'

He looked at her, wanting to have this thing out once and for all, but instead of answering his question she stood up and said politely, 'I think I need a shower. Could I?'

'Fine.' Two can play at this game, he thought, and I'll be damned if I end up being the one to create a scene over this. That made him feel better, and he stood up and headed up the staircase, hearing the light pad of her tread behind him.

Frankly, he told himself, the whole thing is destined to be short-lived anyway. I might be drawn to her physically, but let's not forget that this woman has the capacity to push me to the limits of my endurance.

He handed her a towel and lounged against the doorframe, watching her as she undressed in front of him, with an expression that veered touchingly between embarrassment and nonchalance.

The flashes of nudity before she disappeared into the shower cubicle were like the teasing provocation of a striptease, and he pulled open the shower door and looked at her.

'Mind if I join you?' he heard himself ask, and she muttered something indistinct, which he decided to interpret as an enthusiastic and positive response.

He undressed and stepped in beside her. How the hell, he thought, could he fail to be turned on by the sight of that body under the shower, warm water spraying off her?

He forgot the antagonism he had felt minutes before. He forgot the fact that he had already decided she frustrated him.

'Is this another new experience for you?' he asked huskily, and when she nodded he felt a surge of sheer delight flood through him. He switched off the shower, lathered his hands with soap and massaged her body, starting with her neck and moving very slowly down, over her breasts, playing with her nipples, breathing hoarsely as he felt them harden against the pads of his thumbs.

Whatever thoughts had been going through her head no longer were. He could tell. He could tell from the flush on her cheeks and from her breathing, which was coming in little gasps. She might retreat behind those barricades whenever she felt threatened, but nothing could hide the fact that she wanted him as much as he wanted her, and that turned him on.

He concentrated on her breasts. He loved the feel of them, small and pointed and responsive to his touch. Her nipples were large and beautifully well defined. He gazed at them and his own breathing quickened.

'Touch me,' he muttered into her ear, feeling his hardness pulsate as her hand wrapped around him and began rubbing with exquisite rhythm. There was a pounding in his ears, but he wasn't going to rush this, even though he could tell by her little moans and the feverish squirming of her body that she could hardly control herself.

She clasped her fingers into his hair, pulling his head down to hers so that she could kiss him. Her body was still slippery from the water. It was like caressing silk. He kissed her neck, and groaned with pleasure when she demanded more, pushing his head down until his searching mouth found her nipple. Then she arched back, thrusting her breast fully into his mouth. He could hear her small exclamations of pleasure as he suckled hard on it, biting, licking, feeling it stiff in his mouth.

They had backed against the tiled wall. His brain felt like cotton wool. Seeing her like this, open to his every touch, aroused him in a way that almost physically hurt. He ran his hands along her stomach, around to her back, then between her legs, rubbing her rhythmically, turned on by her fevered excitement.

She had parted her legs slightly, a temptation too powerful to resist. He kissed her stomach, then held her waist in both his hands and pulled her body to him, pressing the damp tendrils of hair between her legs against his mouth, exploring with his tongue. He felt giddy with heat and desire as she responded to him, guiding his head so that his tongue could find those secret places that gave her the greatest pleasure. He could feel the level of her excitement rising higher and higher until her body tensed against his mouth and then slackened.

'You're beautiful,' he whispered huskily, knowing that she wouldn't hear him. And she was. Exquisite. Enough to drive a man mad. He stood up on shaking legs and guided her hand back to where his arousal confirmed what he thought. As she stroked him harder, he felt the powerful rush of his climax. When the shudders finally left his body, he turned on the shower again, feeling gloriously refreshed as the water cascaded over him.

Afterwards he watched, depressed, as she got dressed and he slung on his dressing gown.

'Shall we continue the conversation here?' he asked, and she shook her head. 'Why not? Afraid that you might not be able to concentrate on the issue at hand?'

'No. Afraid that *you* might not.'

He grinned reluctantly, wishing with frustration that she didn't have to leave quite so soon. Actually, he wished that she just hadn't bothered to get dressed. The only time he ever seemed to see her with all her defences down and her face lucidly transparent was when she was naked, when desire melted her composure.

'You do realise that you're forcing me into the position of having to make another cup of coffee?' he said over his shoulder as they went downstairs. 'Making drinkable cups of coffee has never been my forte.'

'That and riding horses?'

'That was below the belt!'

'Well, if nothing else, you certainly seem to be quick off the mark when it comes to recuperation.'

With his back to her, her voice was as warm and as velvety as the shower they had shared, and once in the kitchen he took his time with the coffee. Doing a thorough job, he told himself, aware somewhere deep down that really he was simply putting off her moment of departure, putting off a conversation which he did not particularly want to have but could see no way to avoid.

'So...I take it that you're going to employ this perfect human being for the job?' he asked a few minutes later as he sipped his coffee. He looked at her evenly over the rim of the cup. She had done a half-hearted job of drying her hair with the towel, and it was still damp and hung around her face in long strands. Her face, bare of any make-up, looked even younger and more exposed. He had known women whose looks had been far more seductive than hers, but none who could instantly fill him with such sudden, overpowering desire.

'I think so, yes.' She wasn't looking at him. She was fiddling with the handle of her cup.

'I see. And you're absolutely sure that this is the right man for the job?' Of course she was damn well sure. She wouldn't have spent ten minutes praising him earlier on otherwise, would she?

'I don't think we're going to find anyone more suitable.'

'Right.'

'I'm not really cut out for life as a GP,' she muttered in such a low voice that he had to lean forward to catch what she was saying. 'I've been too accustomed to the rush of adrenaline that I get from working in a big hospital. A sense of continuing challenge. Not that being here hasn't shown me certain advantages. It's much more relaxing than life in London.'

She looked at him, challenging him to argue, but what

could he say? His vocal chords seemed to have become paralysed. Was this how it felt to have the ground yanked from under your feet? And how could he complain? What right did he have? What was she doing except the task she had come to do in the first place? Find a suitable replacement for her father, do her filial duty? He cursed the day he'd had that brainwave of getting in touch with her. His mouth felt stiff and there was a ball of anger inside him, lying there like a curled fist.

'Addicted to a life of high stress,' he said coolly. 'Difficult, I suppose, to take off the career hat once it's firmly planted on your head.'

'I suppose so,' she agreed with a little shrug, while her eyes remained riveted on the floral pattern on the cup. He realised that she hadn't actually met his eyes once since they had left the bedroom. Something was going through that head of hers. Something. But what? She kept her feelings hidden and, by God, he wanted to prise her open like a nut, and take out the thoughts she was keeping from him.

'And how does your father feel about you leaving?' His voice was harsh. 'Or perhaps you've ceased to care now that you've sorted out your priorities.'

'That's not fair!'

Lots of things aren't fair, James thought savagely. You were in my arms half an hour ago and now you're sitting here, telling me about your replacement, telling me that you're off. So what's fair about that?

The arguments he had convincingly told himself when he had first felt that treacherous flare of attraction—that she was very far removed from his ideal woman, that she was the challenge of the highbrow female, a challenge that he had once tasted and rejected—were nowhere on the horizon. All he felt was some terrible knot of emotion that had somehow wrapped itself around his head and was playing havoc with his thoughts.

He would have to get himself together.

'When exactly do you intend to leave?'

'As soon as possible.' She still had her eyes lowered so that he couldn't even begin to read the expression on her face, but her voice didn't waver. Some thought process, he realised, had taken place, had given her this grim determination to retreat back into her shell, and for the life of him he couldn't figure it out. How could he argue against something that he just couldn't figure out?

'There's a medical conference in New York in a fortnight's time,' she was saying, in the same low voice. 'Paediatricians and child specialists from all around the world are going to be there. I hope I shall be gone by then.' She took a deep breath. 'Father understands. It helps that he seems to like Derek Clayton. Anyway, he's always known that I would leave, sooner or later. I don't belong here. I never did.'

'And you belong in London?' James said in a voice laced with sarcasm. He had a thread of suspicion that there was some weird discordance between what she was saying and what she really wanted to say, but what? James didn't know but he knew that she was making sure, for reasons of her own, that her barriers remained impenetrable.

'London's alive. Buzzing.' She looked across the table at him. 'How did your marriage end, James?'

'What does that have to do with anything?'

'I'm curious.' She looked at him with her calm, intelligent eyes, masking those contradictory emotions, ones he couldn't even guess at. It was a real struggle to return the look, because every muscle in his body felt stretched to breaking point. It was ridiculous. Absurd. He was a man of the world and yet here he was, confronting this situation with all the stomach-churning, impotent fury of a child denied a toy. It was humiliating.

Oh, well, he thought viciously, we can't have any of that curiosity going unsatisfied, can we?

Was that all she felt for him? Curiosity and desire? Was that *it*? The thought that he might want more was so sudden that he had a brief de-railed feeling, before he pushed the thought out of his head. What more could he possibly want from a relationship with Ellie Mills? Or from any woman, come to that? He had had enough of commitment to last a lifetime. He wasn't about to go down that road again. Talking about Antonia might just help reinforce that.

'I've already told you. She lived for her job. For her, I was the perfect catch because I was as high-flying as she was, and for a while it worked. Two people in demanding careers, a very hectic social life. Who knows? Maybe we might well still be at it if we'd continued to live in London.'

No chance, he thought to himself. The cracks had already started appearing even there and they were the sort of cracks that couldn't be sorted out by turning a blind eye.

'But then I had to return here and Antonia hated it,' he went on. 'She loathed the anonymity of country life.' He shrugged dismissively. 'And she could well have had something there. I've been giving quite a bit of thought to returning to London, letting Frank take over the stud farm...' He looked at her from under his lashes to see how this revelation was going down, but her face was studiously blank.

'Why on earth would you want to do that?' Ellie asked. 'I thought you enjoyed being out here in the country.'

'Yes, well, the country is fine,' James replied tersely, 'but as a lifelong diet it just gets a bit too much for me.'

'Oh, I see.'

She didn't looked thrilled, he thought angrily. In fact,

she looked positively put out. What the hell was going on here? he wondered. How could someone change colours so rapidly and with so little warning? He felt as though he had left the play during the interval, only to return and find that he was watching the second half of a completely different performance.

'Naturally, I wouldn't live in the centre of London…' Did she look relieved at that? He was watching her intently—too intently. Maybe he was beginning to see things that just weren't there. Yes, he decided, that was it. For some reason, he had begun reading all sorts of things into her responses. He relaxed back in his chair and half closed his eyes with sudden relief.

All she'd told him, after all, was that she'd found a replacement.

'Somewhere just outside, I think. Perhaps Richmond. Maybe even as far out as Guildford.'

'James…'

Something in her tone of voice made him open his eyes and look at her. She hadn't raised the level of her voice, but there was a firmness there and he felt the knot in his stomach tighten.

'I think there's something we need to talk about…' She wasn't looking at him as she said this. She was back to concentrating on her coffee-cup. 'I can't really see the point of us…carrying on with this relationship… I mean, I shall be returning to London to live…' Her voice drifted off, but her mouth was set in a stubborn line.

James didn't think that he had ever been given the 'Dear John' speech by a woman in his life before. But that wasn't the point. The point was that what she was saying seemed to have jumped at him from out of the blue. He felt a deathly chill run through him, and he knew that the lines of his face were rigid and set.

'It was inevitable that you would return to London at some point,' he said with what he considered to be a remarkable level of cool reason in his voice. 'This was never going to be a permanent posting.' He paused, wondering how to phrase the logical continuation of his line of thought without sounding desperate. Because desperate was something he had never been in his life before, and he certainly wasn't desperate now. A little taken aback, sure. But that was because all of this was so entirely unexpected.

'That doesn't necessarily mean that this has got to end.' He tried to inject a certain amount of persuasion into his voice, mixed with jocularity, and she threw him a quick, uneasy glance. 'I mean,' he continued, in the same tone of voice, 'there's a more than strong chance that I shall return to London to work, anyway. Like I said, I've been considering handing over the reins here to Frank. He'd like nothing better than managing this stud farm without having to refer every decision to me. It's what he's been doing for time immemorial anyway!'

He managed something along the lines of a laugh. 'This latest episode with the horse has only brought home to me my own limitations in running the place. Really, I came back here after my father died to carry on the farm, which I thought I could do without forsaking all my other business interests, but quite frankly it's more than time that we parted company. I still have a few bruises to back me up on this one.' He smiled, but she didn't smile back.

'It wouldn't work,' she said gently. 'Even if you did return to London.'

That chill was growing into a freezing wind blowing through his body.

'Why not?' he demanded, hating himself for persevering, but incapable of shrugging and walking away. He looked at her aggressively and he could feel her cringe back, even though she remained perfectly, infuriatingly, maddeningly still. It was like talking to a bloody brick wall. 'Why the hell not?'

'Maybe we should carry on this discussion another time.'

'We'll damn well finish it here and now!' he shouted. 'Look,' he continued in a calmer voice. 'All I want to know is, why this sudden change of mind?' He would have ventured a smile, but he had a suspicion that it might alarm rather than reassure her. 'Don't you enjoy what we've got? I know I enjoy making love to you.'

'That's hardly the point, is it?' she said flatly.

Isn't it? he wondered, bewildered.

'The point is, yes, I *do* enjoy making love to you. I don't want you to see this as an insult to your masculine pride. The fact is that I've been giving this a great deal of thought and I'm really not prepared to indulge in a relationship that's not going anywhere.' Her voice, which had started off quite bold and self-assured, had sunk to a whisper. In a moment, he thought, seething, she would ask him why he wasn't giving her any support on this one. He could have strangled her.

'What you're saying, in other words, is that this is all a complete waste of time from your point of view.'

'I wouldn't have put it like that...'

'No? How tactful of you.'

'It's just that I'm looking for more out of a relationship,' she said quietly, back to not meeting his eyes, which was just as well because he was very much afraid that although his voice was now under control his eyes might reveal the savagery of his emotions. 'I want commitment, a relationship that's going *somewhere*.'

'I thought you had that and you decided to give it a miss? I recall you saying something about wanting a relationship with no strings attached...' James said with biting sarcasm.

'I can change my mind, can't I? I'm entitled to that,

wouldn't you agree?' Her voice rose a few notches and
there were two red patches on her cheeks. 'You and I,
well, we hit it off on one level, but I'm not your type
any more than you're mine.'

James felt as though he had been punched in the stomach. Was she right? Was it just a case of his masculine
pride taking a little battering? He didn't think that a bit
of wounded ego could be this painful. But then, how
would he know? He'd never found himself in a situation
quite like this before.

'In that case, you're quite right. Why don't you hurry
back to London so that you can find your ideal mate?
Don't forget to have them fill out a questionnaire first,
though. After all, you wouldn't want any inappropriate
character traits slipping through the net, would you?'

'Very funny!' Ellie said hotly, but her eyes were
glazed with tears. Not that that made him feel any less
savage.

'Except it's not, is it? I feel sorry for you, Ellie. Do
you think you can hide behind what you know and never
venture outside to have a look at what you don't?'

'I think I'm entitled to decide whether I want certain
relationships in my life or not!'

So that was it, James thought with grim certainty.
He'd been a fool not to have seen it from the start.
Eleanor Mills, dedicated bookworm, dedicated medical
student, dedicated doctor. So damned dedicated that
she'd never so much as peered outside the little world
she'd created for herself. He really did feel sorry for her.

Poor woman. Comes over to Ireland on her errand of
mercy, having been forced into it, and she feels desire
for the first time. She has a glimpse of what lies outside
the room she's barricaded herself into. Who could blame
her for taking advantage of it? Who could blame her for
wanting to get back to her sane little world now that she
had tried what was on offer?

She used me! he thought, relishing the knife in the wound, twisting it so that it hurt even more.

Emotions that he'd never felt before poured through him like a black, thick stream of bile. He couldn't identify any one of them. The torrent was too strong. He just knew that they left an acrid, bitter taste in his mouth, however much he was trying to rise above them and see her for the undoubtedly sad creature that she was. Better to have discovered the sort of woman that she was now, rather than later.

Her hair had almost completely dried. Blonde again. He would never see that hair fall in a curtain along the side of her face again.

'Well, what can I say but good luck?' He stood up and she followed suit, looking a little dazed by the suddenness of his movement. 'I'm only overjoyed that I've been of some use.' He strode towards the front door with his fists bunched in his pockets, not bothering to glance behind him to see whether she was following or not.

'What do you mean?' she asked when they were at the front door, and he looked down at her with a sneer.

'Oh, you know what I mean,' he drawled. 'You had your bit of fun with me and it's put you in just the right frame of mind to go back to what you had.'

'That's cruel!' Ellie muttered, her face distressed. 'You make it sound as though I...used you...'

James shrugged. 'Just glad to be of service.'

'You can't tell me that you didn't use me as well,' she said, raising her eyes to his. 'You yourself said that this was a relationship with no strings attached! You're just taken aback because you weren't the one to finish it!'

No more kisses on that mouth, he thought. No more soaring feelings of touching the sky whenever he reached out and traced his finger along the contours of her face.

'You could at least give it a try...' He heard what sounded like desperation in his voice and was disgusted by his own, treacherous weakness.

'James...'

The answer was written in that one word. She had no need to say anything further, and he pulled open the front door.

'Forget it. You deserve the destiny that you get, and good luck with it.'

He still had to drop her back home, a task which he didn't relish. It was a drive done in complete silence. She looked out of the window, watching the black landscape slip past, and he drove as quickly as he could. And he didn't look at her once as she opened the car door, hesitating for just a few seconds.

He didn't look at her because he knew that one more patronising, pitying word from her would send him over the edge. So he kept his eyes resolutely averted and as soon as she had slipped her key into the front door he reversed the car and drove away, accelerating to what seemed a reckless speed on the short, narrow road back.

His eyes saw the road ahead; his mind saw that vulnerable face, with its ever changing shadows of expression. He told himself that he was well rid of her. He told himself that she had been spot-on when she'd said that he was simply suffering from a case of wounded masculine pride.

He screeched to a halt outside his house and left the engine running. He didn't get out of the car. He remained where he was, killing the headlights and sitting there, staring.

Okay, so he had wanted her. All this stuff he was feeling was just a matter of frustrated desire. He banged the steering wheel hard and gritted his teeth together.

Life would be infinitely easier without Ellie Mills around. He could get back to his work without his mind constantly feeling as though it had been put through a wringer. He could concentrate on things once again. He would open his mind to the possibility of another woman, someone more suitable, someone who didn't come equipped with an array of complicated personal problems. In fact, someone who didn't think too much at all. Thinking was a dangerous pastime. Unless it was to do with work.

He only realised that he had spent over an hour sitting in that car in the dark when he looked at the digital clock on the dashboard. Then he went inside, slamming the front door behind him.

CHAPTER NINE

GETTING back into the routine of London was a bit like slipping back on a pair of shoes you hadn't worn for a while. Not as comfortable as the slippers you'd left behind, but comfortable enough once you got the hang of them.

Ellie submerged herself into hospital life again, picking up from where she had left off almost as if she had never gone away in the first place, almost as though those intervening weeks had been nothing more than a dream. After a month, her flat, which had initially felt cold and impersonal in comparison with the surprisingly companionable warmth of her father's house, was once again home. Somewhere she returned to simply lay her bones for brief rests before the hectic schedule began once more.

It was a schedule she preferred not to think about too much. When she did think about it, about her life, she was overcome by the breathless, claustrophobic feeling of being caught on a treadmill. She had never, ever imagined that she could return to small-town living and actually prefer it, but now every aspect of London life invited comparisons.

The air wasn't as clean, the people were too focused and unfriendly, her powerful job at the hospital did not allow her time to breathe, her flat lacked personality. Even her friends, with whom she had made a concerted effort to re-establish contact, seemed wrapped up in their own little bubbles, selfishly assuming that their own lives and their own problems were all that anyone could possibly be interested in.

And James. Most of all, Ellie tried not to think about James. It was impossible. The memory of him clung to her like fine gossamer, sabotaging all her efforts to banish it through hard work and a mind too exhausted to think about anything.

She relived that last night they had spent together over and over and over, remembering how she had felt, after that shared shower, that glorious shared shower, when she'd realised that she had fallen in love with him. The feeling of panic. *How could she have fallen in love with James Kellern? How could she?* Like suddenly finding herself in a room with all the walls closing in. Just so long as she had explained away her response to him as nothing more than desire, she had been in control. More or less. But love was something quite different. She couldn't afford to fall in love with him, because that was the road to certain self-destruction.

James Kellern was a self-confessed cynic when it came to relationships with women and she was too old, too settled, maybe even too frightened to indulge in a passion which would leave her wounded for the rest of her life. The line between loving and needing was a fine one, and the line between need and dependency was even finer. To depend on a man like James Kellern would be as foolish as depending on the seas to be forever calm, and she was too sensible to try to tame stormy waters.

Still, when she spoke to her father on the telephone now, she had to bite back her curiosity to know what James was doing, saying, thinking, feeling. When, on three occasions, her father mentioned his name, she feigned indifference, but she knew that her heartbeat had quickened and her face was hot.

Did he ever think of her at all? Or had she been shoved into that box labelled 'The Past', a little collection of memories of the one that got away? Something he dipped into now and again with rueful amusement? Or maybe relief?

It was a little over four weeks since she had seen him and she wished that she could sleep away the next six months and awaken, refreshed, to find that all the memories had been put away, that time had done its thing and cleared her head.

Now, emerging from her reverie, Ellie looked at her watch and saw that it was seven o'clock. It was also her birthday. Henry was taking her out the following evening for a goodbye meal. Funny how a little stay in a remote Irish village could change all the characters in the play. Henry was leaving London to establish a practice on his own just outside York, where he had grown up. So they would be celebrating her birthday and his decision to quit London, and Ellie knew that she would have to smile and smile through it all, even if she felt like bursting into tears.

She should have left work at four o'clock for her time off, which she had intended to put to industrious use by going shopping, cooking herself a meal—including a birthday cake—and watching a video.

But naturally she had been needed at the hospital. This invariably happened whenever Ellie planned to leave early, but her optimism, somehow, never faltered when the arrangement was made again.

Normally, she accepted her cancelled time off with a resigned shrug. Now, as she took a taxi back to her flat, she felt for the first time a small stirring of resentment. When she was old and grey, and at the top of her formidable career, would she look back and say with delight, 'Thank heavens I spent all my time working'?

And that small stirring of resentment frightened her. Devotion to her job, beyond the call of duty, was something she had always taken for granted. It was something she needed. What, she thought worriedly as she pottered around in the kitchen later, would be the next step? Clock-watching? She couldn't afford that in her job.

She viciously sliced some spring onions and then prepared to do the same to a few mushrooms.

Everything seemed to have changed around her, and she had never been prepared for upheaval. She had worked hard all her life, set herself goals and achieved them. Control had been her way of dealing with a childhood spent in awe and trepidation of her father. Gradually she had built up her shell, until it had become part and parcel of her character. Now, nothing seemed certain any more. Her emotions were no longer in one place, her mind was no longer reliable. It kept wandering off and there seemed to be nothing she could do to prevent it. Henry's decision to leave London was just one more thing in her rapidly changing world.

She began making a sauce for some pasta and felt very lonely at the thought of seeing another birthday in on her own. Just her, her thoughts, and her dissatisfaction.

It occurred to her, as she sat down at the dining-room table, elaborately set for one, that she should have invited one of her friends over for supper. Or maybe the whole lot of them. Had a party. Drunk huge amounts of wine, told jokes, laughed loudly. Except, she thought, she wasn't like that, not at all, which was probably why the idea was only now occurring to her instead of two weeks earlier, when it would have been easy to arrange.

Still, there *was* wine in the fridge, and so what if she was on her own? It was still her birthday, wasn't it?

Her meal over, she cleared the table, studiously returning it to its former polished glory, but drawing the line at washing all the dishes. Then she poured herself a glass of wine and carried it and the bottle into the small front room, where she kicked off her shoes, dimmed the lights, switched on some music and prepared to do her damnedest to enjoy the evening.

Which, two glasses later, was looking rather rosier than it had earlier on. She wondered whether it would be positively glowing if she finished off the bottle completely. Or if she would go past the rosy stage and enter the nightmarish world of the maudlin drunk. Having never before consumed enough alcohol to be bothered by the question, she looked at the bottle for an answer, and was about to go for it when the doorbell rang.

'Damn,' Ellie muttered under her breath. It occurred to her that she didn't want company after all. She didn't want to sit down and make conversation with anyone. She just wanted, on this once-a-year day, to lie in complete self-indulgence on the sofa, with the lights turned down, and wallow in her sorrow.

Most of all, she hoped that it wouldn't be hospital business. Generally, they phoned if she was needed, but very occasionally one of her fellow consultants, Gregory Rowlands, who lived a few streets away, would drop by to discuss something with her.

She didn't really feel as though her mind was up to discussing anything with intelligence. It very nearly occurred to her to pretend that she wasn't in, but force of habit prevented that.

Still, there was no need to be jovial. She pulled open the door and saw James Kellern outside.

Her split second of utter confusion seemed to last hours. But a second was all the time it took to absorb his tall, lean figure, casual in a pair of jeans and an oatmeal sweater. All the time it took to feel the masculine potency of his presence. It was as though her thoughts, raging inside her ever since she had left Ireland, had somehow diabolically summoned up his presence.

Then she blinked and said tightly, 'You! What are you doing here?'

Before, she had felt languid, melancholy. Now, every

nerve in her body was stretched taut and her stomach was coiled with tension.

'I'm here on instructions from your father,' James told her. He made no move to come inside the flat, but on the other hand he didn't exactly look as though he was about to turn around and depart. His body was casually indolent, as were his eyes.

'My father?' Ellie shook her head. 'He's all right, isn't he? I spoke to him myself this morning. He called at the crack of dawn to wish me a happy birthday.' She had always, in the past, received birthday cards from him. Never a call. She had been surprised and touched.

'He asked me to give you this.' James straightened and held out a little box to her.

Ellie took the box from him, concentrating hard on opening it while her body was acutely aware of him. It was a diamond brooch, with a note from her father explaining that it had belonged to her mother. She turned it over in her hands, more moved than she could remember feeling at any gesture her father had ever made towards her, and then raised her eyes to James.

'Thank you for delivering it,' she said evenly. 'Though I'm not sure why he didn't let me know that you were coming.' *She would give anything just to reach out and touch him. Why couldn't things have been different? Why couldn't she have been more reckless, or James less bitter about women? In an ideal world, they would have met when they were both young enough not to be afraid of adventure. Or her, at any rate.*

'He wanted to surprise you,' he drawled, leaning against the doorframe and thus more or less ruling out the possibility of closing the door in his face.

'Well, he has. I shall call him in the morning and thank him.' She paused, looked at him with a deliberately unfocused gaze and said politely, 'Was that all?'

'What are you doing on your birthday?' he asked with leisurely interest.

'Nothing.'

'Shame.'

'Why is it a shame?' She didn't want to prolong this conversation but on the other hand she couldn't resist the impulse to keep him there, just so she could feed her hunger for him. 'I was rather enjoying myself, actually.' Ho, ho, ho.

'Have you eaten?'

'Yes.'

'This is proving to be a very difficult conversation,' he said. 'Rather monosyllabic. I realise that things might be a bit…uncomfortable between us, but we're both adults.' He bent down and retrieved a bottle which she had not noticed on the ground. 'I brought around some champagne on the off chance that you were alone.'

Ellie looked at it, and had to stop herself from searching for a hidden meaning behind his gesture.

'Come in.'

She reached to switch on the lights and he said quickly, 'Leave them. It's more restful like this.'

Ellie doubted that she could feel restful in the presence of James Kellern, whatever the circumstances, but she let her hand fall and went into the kitchen, to emerge with two champagne flutes.

'So,' he said, looking at her as they went into the sitting room. 'How have you been? Enjoying London?'

'Absolutely.' She then proceeded to tell him precisely why she was enjoying London so much, which sounded like a list of precisely all the reasons why she wasn't. The breakneck work schedule, the buzz. She even waxed lyrical on the subject of the crowds, which she hated, but which were now glamorised into a teeming mass of thrilling individuals leading exciting lives.

By the end of which, she had only managed to drink

one glass of the champagne. At this rate she would be here for hours, she thought, lying about her life and trying hard not to stare at him as though he were a life-raft in the middle of a stormy sea.

'Father mentioned that you went across to visit him a few days ago,' she said, making conversation. 'Thank you. It's nice to know that someone's keeping an eye on him.'

'Yes,' he drawled, reclining back on the sofa, glass in hand. 'Between Brenda and myself, your father need never be short of company.'

'Brenda?'

'Bush. Widow. Age sixty-something. Member of the opera society and—what a coincidence—also of the bridge club. She's been making sure that your father's fed and watered.'

'I see.' Ellie smiled with genuine warmth. Her father had not talked about Brenda Bush—at least only in passing. No wonder he had sounded so relaxed and happy when she had spoken to him recently.

'Surprised?'

'Happy for him. I'm amazed that he never got around to it sooner. I would have thought he would be quite a catch for some of those village women.'

'Better late than never, though, don't you think?' He gave her a long, curious look, then looked away. 'No birthday cake?' he asked conversationally, changing the subject with a speed and fluency that she had grown accustomed to.

Ellie hesitated fractionally, and he said, with a beam, 'I saw it in the kitchen. Bring it out. Might as well cut it with me. I can't think of anything worse than cutting your own birthday cake without an audience, even an audience of one. Even if that one happens to be me.' Jovial voice, but still that concealed expression which made her nervous and jumpy.

She made an instant decision, brought the cake out, with two plates, two forks and a knife, and deposited it with some embarrassment on the table in front of the fireplace. She had stuck three candles on it. Three candles on a cake shaped like a dog and iced with black spots. Very sad when you thought of it.

'*One Hundred and One Dalmations* is one of my favourite movies,' she said defensively, as though he had remarked on the cake, which he hadn't. She picked up the knife, ready to cut it, but he told her that she had to light the candles first. *And* blow them out. *And* make a wish. She wondered if it would be a waste of a wish to wish that he weren't here. Did he feel sorry for her? Did he imagine that she would sink into a maudlin torpor if she was left on her own?

She then wondered whether her father had read the depression in her voice when she had spoken to him on the telephone. A few months ago, she would have laughed off the idea, but things had subtly changed between them and now she wasn't too sure. He had become more astute, at least as far as she was concerned.

After she had blown out the candles, she glanced up at him and, as he leaned forward, their eyes met. Disturbingly, she found that she couldn't look away. Breathing was a little difficult too. And the subdued lighting wasn't helping. What was needed was fluorescent lights. She desperately wished that she'd had that party. But then, she hadn't known that this would be the outcome of her planned night of solitary enjoyment, had she?

James leaned forward towards her. To do what? She couldn't think. He leaned closer and then suddenly yelled, 'Aagh! Oh, my God!'

'What?' Ellie sprang back in horror.

'My back!' His face was contorted and she hurried over to him, but he brushed her aside. 'No!'

'I'm a doctor!'

'I…it's happened before!' He made an attempt to stand up and then collapsed back onto the sofa. 'It's not serious.'

'Let me have a look,' Ellie commanded. 'I may not specialise in backs, but I'll be able to tell you what the problem is. See whether we should get you to a hospital.'

She was standing right next to him now, but her professional hat was very securely in place.

'No!' He edged away. 'Please. I'd really rather just wait this one out. Like I said, it's not the first time it's happened.'

'What did your doctor say the last time?'

'Recurrence of an old injury,' James muttered under his breath. 'Riding injury.'

'You fell from your horse? Again? You really are very accident-prone!'

'No, no. That last fall must have done it. Brought back this damned—aagh!—dislocated back of mine.'

Ellie folded her arms and looked at him worriedly. She didn't like this business of not examining him. He was the very last man in the world she would ever have chosen as a patient—last time had been bad enough—but right now it felt uncomfortably like professional misconduct.

'I'll be fine,' he insisted, watching her from what looked like a very awkward position, his hand on his lower back.

'How,' Ellie asked, suddenly waking up to the practicalities of the situation, 'are you going to travel back? Did you bring your car with you? If you have, then I suggest you leave it here and get a cab back to your apartment.'

'I don't think I could make the ride,' James said heavily. He winced again and pressed his back with the palm of his hand. 'If I could just lie on a firm bed…?'

'*Whose* firm bed did you have in mind?' Ellie asked, trying to keep calm in the face of rising panic.

'Look, I know it's damned inconvenient, but…' He tried to stand and made a fairly poor job of it. He did, she thought with anxiety, look pretty bad. She only wished that he'd let her examine him.

'Could you stop staring at me so suspiciously and help me to a bed? Any bed?' He was hunched over slightly, and when she approached him, he leaned heavily against her.

'You can lie on the bed in the spare bedroom,' Ellie told him, 'until you feel up to leaving.'

Ellie had lifted enough people in her time for her to acquire a certain amount of strength, but James was tall and well-built, and even though he was shuffling she could still feel his weight pressing against her, and was very aware of the position of his hand, dangling just above her breast.

She helped him onto the bed, where he lay, seemingly exhausted.

'Perhaps I could massage it,' she felt compelled to suggest, standing over him, frowning. 'I probably have some cream in the medicine cupboard.'

'No need.'

Thank God, she thought. 'You mean it's feeling better already?'

'No,' he sighed in a low voice. 'I'm sorry about this, but it might take a day or so…'

'*A day or so?*'

'If past experience is anything to go by.' He gave her a wounded look, as though quibbling over such a trivial thing was an insult, given the fact that he had put his back out.

'B-but…' Ellie stammered. 'A day or so…?'

James looked at her from under his lashes. 'It's not a problem, is it? I mean, the spare bedroom *is* spare, isn't it? Naturally, if you expect company, I could see whether I could make it to my place in the back of a taxi, but in the past immediate rest has always been the best way to get rid of this little problem.' He laughed, but weakly. 'I really would rather not do myself any further injury.'

'No.' She sighed in resignation. She didn't like the idea of having him stay under her roof, even if it was only for a couple of days, but that was because she didn't trust herself. She didn't trust her emotions to give her the backing she needed when he was around.

It was hardly as though she didn't trust him. For a start, he had been perfectly polite this evening. No suggestive remarks anywhere, no arguments. The perfect guest, in fact. And now…well, it was hardly as though he was a threat when he obviously could barely walk.

'Would you like something to drink? Or to eat, for that matter?'

'Well, we never did make it to the birthday cake, did we?'

So she brought him a slice of the birthday cake and a cup of coffee, and then retired to the chair by the window while he ate.

'Nice cake,' he said, his appetite clearly unaffected by his back.

'If a bit sweet.'

'That's because the ratio of icing to cake is approximately fifty-fifty,' he said, depositing the plate on the side of the bed and then making an effort to drink the coffee, but in the end giving up. 'I apologise for such a dismal ending to your birthday, but…' He shrugged in a Gallic way, and Ellie stood up briskly.

'Forget it.' She gathered up the plate and the cup and headed to the door. 'Give me a shout if it gets any worse,' she said, turning towards him. 'There's a light by the bed if you want to read, and some magazines, though they're probably not to your taste.' She switched off the top light just as he turned on the bedside lamp. Instantly, she felt a stab of something very unprofessional, and she hurried out of the room, giving the door a sharp tug behind her.

She drifted off to sleep two hours later, thinking about him in the room next to hers, and picked up the thought the minute she opened her eyes the following morning.

When she went to check on him, she found him still in bed, though awake, and half-naked.

'I see you've managed to get out of your shirt,' she said, nervously averting her eyes. She stepped across to the curtains and yanked them open, so that what sunlight there was filtered into the room. There was no point in holding a conversation in the shadows. That just made her feel at a disadvantage.

'With great difficulty,' James told her, following her with his eyes.

'How are you feeling?'

'Not much better, I'm afraid. Any chance of some painkillers?'

'I think you should let me have a look at that back of yours. Then we can decide whether you need to go to Casualty.'

'What are your plans for today?' he asked, neatly avoiding the question.

'I have a few bits and pieces to do,' Ellie told him vaguely. 'Do you think that you could rouse yourself for some breakfast?'

'You might have to feed it to me,' he said in a subdued voice, which was an idea she found not at all appealing.

But what she could do? If she didn't know better, she would have thought that he was malingering, but James Kellern was simply not the sort of man to tolerate ill health, and anyway, why would he feign a bad back?

She returned to the bedroom fifteen minutes later with some toast and scrambled egg and helped him into a comfortable sitting position. When she deposited the tray in front of him and turned to leave, he said, rather more insistently, 'It's awfully uncomfortable moving. Could you...?'

Ellie shot him an exasperated look, and perched awkwardly next to him on the bed. 'This is ridiculous,' she muttered. 'Are you sure you're not overplaying the pain?' She didn't want to mention his last unfortunate accident, but she would have liked to point out that he hadn't been too bad then, had he? 'If it's still so severe that you can't manage to feed yourself, then you really need to get to the hospital. This sort of thing can be exacerbated by being ignored.'

She fed him a mouthful of scrambled egg, leaning over so that the whole mess couldn't spill on the sheets. She felt her breasts push against her shirt and kept her eyes firmly fixed on his face. With the smallest of movements, he could reach out and touch them. She remembered what that felt like, his hands, his mouth moving over her nipples. She had to force her hand to remain steady.

He made no move to help himself. He reclined in a half-heartedly propped position on the pillows, allowing her to put spoonfuls of toast and egg into his mouth, while she felt increasingly uncomfortable with every passing minute. And in between mouthfuls he chatted to her, forcing her to respond.

'Perhaps,' he suggested, when the exercise was finally over, 'you could massage my back now. Last night, it was just too painful, but I think...'

Would she ever leave the flat? she wondered. She fetched the cream and returned to find that he was now lying on his stomach. From what she could see, his nudity didn't just extend from the waist up. She felt faintly alarmed at this, and her hands, when they rested on his lower back, only increased her uneasiness.

She began rubbing on cream and after a while said that she couldn't detect any undue swelling.

'Still hurts like hell,' he said, sounding rather relaxed. 'A bit lower. Please.'

She was aware, during this process, that he was making small talk to her, chatting about her father, and she could hear herself responding in what seemed a very normal voice, but her eyes were riveted on his torso and what her eyes couldn't see her imagination happily filled in. Three inches lower, and she would touch his naked body completely, feel its smooth hardness under her fingers. She could feel perspiration forming a fine film over her. In a minute, she'd be in a trance-like state.

'Right.' She stood up and re-covered the tube. 'I really must go. I've got lots of things to do. Feel free to phone for a taxi when you're up to leaving. No need to wait for me to return.'

James shifted so that he was lying on his back and looking at her. 'That felt good,' he murmured lazily, and she flushed. 'Of course I'll leave if I feel up to it. I don't want to get in your way. But, just in case I'm still here when you return, is there any chance you could get me today's copy of the *FT*? I also like to browse through the *Daily Telegraph* and *The Times*.'

'Anything else?' She arched her eyebrows. 'What about a few good books and a pair of pyjamas?'

'I never sleep in pyjamas.' He grinned at her, enjoying her discomfort at this little shared confidence.

She couldn't tell, when she was finally out of the flat, whether she was irritated, embarrassed, nervous or a combination of all three. With a generous dash of charming apprehension thrown in to top it all off.

And being outside in the cool air did nothing to dispel any of those feelings. She ran through the shops, stocking up on food and essentials, while her mind busied itself in other directions. It was as if all thought patterns led right back to James Kellern, however hard she tried to distance herself from his image.

She dreaded returning to the flat to find him still there, but on the other hand the thought that he might have left in her absence sent waves of dismay and disappointment crashing through her. She didn't know what she wanted. What *did* she want? Peace of mind?

When, several hours later, she opened the door to her flat to find his jacket still slung over the sofa, she expelled a long breath of shuddering pleasure, then immediately chastised herself for the reaction. Did she *enjoy*, she wondered, having her pain rubbed into her like salt in a wound? Every minute with him here, under the same roof, was a little agony, so why should she be pleased to know that he hadn't gone?

She rattled about in the kitchen, putting things away, making herself listen to two messages on her answering machine, one of which was from Henry, reminding her about their date that evening—something which had not entered her head. She wanted to inform James of her presence and subtly let him know that she wasn't rushing in to pay him a courtesy call.

Eventually, though, she went to the spare bedroom, knocked tentatively, and went in armed with the newspapers.

'Sorry,' he said, without much of a note of sincere apology in his voice. 'I think one more night should do the trick. I thought it better not to rush things.' He gave her a winning smile, which she resolutely ignored. 'Ah, you've brought me the newspapers. Great.' He scanned the *Financial Times* and said absent-mindedly, 'I don't want to be a nuisance, but...'

'But you'll swallow your pride and be one anyway?' He threw her a smile of utter charm and Ellie glared

back at him, arms folded. How dared he feel relaxed and
cheery under these circumstances? It annoyed her to
realise that the reason she couldn't respond to the situation with equal good-natured equanimity was that what
she felt for him was like a knife cutting through her. If
she could be as basically indifferent to him as he was to
her, she wouldn't now be standing here, staring at him
and feeling as though her foundations were lying in ruins
around her feet. She would be cheerful, casual and jokey.
He had recovered from her, she thought depressingly,
while for her things had just gone from bad to worse.

'Could you perhaps get me a cup of tea?'

'You're running the risk of making a very bad patient,' Ellie said to him, and he smiled again.

But she fetched him a mug of tea anyway, and also
something light to eat. Three ham and salad sandwiches,
which he accepted with alacrity and ate with dazzling
speed. He patted a space next to him on the bed, which
Ellie disregarded. She did perch on the chair by the window, however, and as he ate and drank, he conversed
on all manner of subjects, like someone deprived of human companionship for decades. Reluctantly, Ellie
found herself responding, and it was only when the shadows were beginning to draw in that she gave a little gasp
and stood up.

'What's up?' James asked conversationally. Ellie regarded him for a long moment. It was here, in this charm
of his, that her downfall had begun. He had talked and
she had responded and after a while it had become very
difficult to maintain a sense of perspective. And later,
when all her detachment had been eroded, she had allowed her defences to be battered down completely. She
had fallen in love with him and here she was again,
reminding herself of her error of judgement, yet doing
nothing about it.

'I'm going out,' she said, withdrawing into herself.

'Where? Anywhere interesting?'

'No.' She walked across to the door, feeling his eyes on her. If she looked at him, he would ask her more questions and it didn't matter whether he was interested in the answers or not. He would ask her them just out of curiosity. So she let herself out, took a deep breath, then spent a very rushed forty-five minutes getting herself ready for Henry's arrival.

She would make sure that the two men didn't meet. Indeed, she would hustle Henry out of the flat before he could open his mouth. True, James was holed up in bed, but that didn't mean that his hearing was impaired, and she had no intention of allowing a day's idleness to turn boredom into a little fun at her expense.

She dressed with particular care, and by the time the doorbell rang she was ready. Midnight-blue dress, straight but in a fine silk that clung to her curves, high heels, and a jacket in the same colour as the dress.

She opened the door to Henry, ready to guide him stealthily out of the door before he could open his mouth, but it was no use. He exclaimed when he saw her, and presented her with a gift-wrapped parcel, shutting the door behind him and talking loudly as he walked through to the sitting room. She followed him with dismay, relieved that at least James, cooped up as he was, was incapable of doing anything—when she heard the sound of a bedroom door, and then footsteps, and then James appeared, face as black as thunder and no sign of a bad back in sight.

CHAPTER TEN

THE two men stared at each other, James with scowling hostility, Henry with the startled look of a goldfish.

James was the first to speak. 'What are you doing here?' This, he thought, was the mildest way of phrasing the question, considering what he was feeling at the moment. What the hell was *Henry* doing here? It was the last thing he had expected and it hurt his jaw just keeping his voice fairly civil.

'Well might I ask you the same question.' But Henry was no longer looking at James when he said that. He was looking at Ellie, who had been watching the two men with alarm. He sounded put out, and she could understand that. He had wanted a quiet evening with her, a suitable and amicable parting of ways. Did he think that she had arranged for James Kellern to be here?

'Ah, Henry, I can explain that.' She sounded like a wife caught by her husband *in flagrante*, rushing in with a litany of phoney excuses. But I'm not, she thought, gathering her aplomb. 'James dropped by yesterday with a present for me from my father...'

'*Yesterday?*' Henry's eyebrows flew up at the piece of information, and she could hear little bells of speculation ringing inside his head.

'Somehow, in the course of the visit, he managed to put his back out and he's been laid up since then in bed.' She shot James a steely look and folded her arms. 'I see,' she said coldly, 'that you've quite recovered.'

James ignored that. He walked into the room and circled Henry as though scrutinising something distasteful and possibly dangerous which was only loosely penned

174

in. 'You still haven't answered my question,' he barked. 'What do you think you're doing here?'

Had she rekindled the flame? The possibility had not occurred to him, but now, seeing Henry in her flat, he wasn't too sure. What if...? He had visions of a new, re-ignited relationship between them and the rage he felt at this made him dizzy. The mere thought of another man coming near her made him feel dizzy. She's mine, he thought with confusing intensity, and, on a calmer level, She's mine now and for the rest of my life. He smiled with disconcerting menace.

'Well, old man,' Henry began, unnerved by James and now wearing the same guilty expression on his face as Ellie had worn earlier on—even though neither of them had anything to feel in the least guilty about. 'I've come to take Ellie out for dinner, as a matter of fact.' He managed a laugh of sorts, which dropped like lead into the aggressive silence in the room. 'Bit of a birthday treat. And we have a few things to talk about as well.'

'Come on, Henry, time to go. You know how popular that restaurant is. If we miss the booking, there goes our table.' She glared at James and protectively linked her arm through Henry's. She refused to act as though she had been caught red-handed in the middle of a criminal act. 'And if you're fully recovered,' she told James coolly, 'then you can see yourself out. I won't expect you to be here when I return.'

She had no idea what his extreme reaction was in aid of, and she had yet to see such a speedy recovery when only minutes before he had been laid up in agony, but now wasn't the time to start musing on the answers to those questions. Right now, all she wanted to do was clear out of the house.

'You're not going anywhere,' James told her conversationally. The rage was dissolving into an implacable feeling of calm. He needed this woman and, dammit, he wasn't going to let her go.

I'm in love with her.

The knowledge weakened and empowered him at the same time. If she and Henry were once again some kind of item, then he would just have to de-itemise them. It was as simple as that. His brain refused to move beyond this.

'Excuse me?'

'Now listen here, old chap,' Henry blustered, clearing his throat, and Ellie didn't know whether to feel even more protective of him and his clumsy embarrassment at the situation, or irritated that he wasn't taking a firmer stance. Thank heavens they hadn't walked in on a burglar in the middle of a job. Lord knew, Henry would probably have apologised for barging in and backed out of the flat.

'No, *you* listen here, *old chap*, I want to have a word with Ellie without you around, so be a good fellow and leave the way you came in, would you?'

'How dare you?' Ellie shouted, her cheeks flaming. 'How *dare* you order Henry around in *my* flat? You have no right to be here. I let you stay last night because you assured me that you couldn't move. Well, movement has returned, so *you* can leave the way *you* came!'

James stepped towards them, his face dark, and Henry, still utterly bewildered, took a step backwards. In the weeks to come, Ellie thought, she might well see the comic side of this little charade.

'Do I have to throw you out, or will you leave while you still have the use of your feet?' The thought of disposing of Henry head-first out of the door was invigorating.

Ellie's mouth dropped open. She was finding it impossible to believe her ears. This all sounded like so much clichéd dialogue from a B-rated action movie, and she was overwhelmed by a feeling of complete unreality. She almost expected to hear some appropriately threatening music in the background.

Henry, whose bewilderment seemed to have given way to alarm, turned to her and said nervously, 'Perhaps I ought to leave, Ellie... I can come back later, when you've had your chat...'

'What chat?' she demanded, facing him. 'James and I have nothing to *chat* about!'

'We damn well have!' James swung her round so that she was looking at him. 'Now, you, out!' He glanced swiftly at Henry, who began retreating towards the front door, and then turned to stare at Ellie.

'Ellie, if you would rather I stayed...' Henry offered, in a last-ditch attempt to be chivalrous, but she shook her head wearily at him.

'No, Henry, it's okay. You shoot off. I'll give you a call later or maybe tomorrow.'

'Well, if you're sure.' She noticed that his voice was more forceful now that his escape route was mapped out.

'Sure. Off you go.'

Which he did, shutting the door behind him and leaving them both staring at one another in silence. The self-righteous anger which she had felt only a short while before, the feeling of calm at the knowledge that James was the intruder, despite the way he had issued commands, had deserted her. She began to wish that Henry hadn't left. She wished that she had scuttled out of the front door with him. She didn't know what was going on. She just knew that she was terrified of her own vulnerability, terrified at the thought of being under the same roof as James when he was in this kind of threatening, unpredictable mood.

'Well, I'm here. You've managed to get rid of Henry, so just say what you have to say and then go.'

James had relaxed. He strolled over to the sofa, sat

down, stretched out his long legs in front of him and proceeded to regard her broodingly from under his lashes.

Which left Ellie in some state of indecision as to what she should do. Sit down? Remain standing? Walk about in a meaningful manner?

She chose to sit, simply because she didn't know whether she could trust her legs to do what they were supposed to do and support her body, when they felt so stupidly wobbly.

'Didn't put up much of a fight, did he?' James drawled with a sneer, once she was seated.

'Which makes him all the more admirable,' Ellie said coldly. She tried very hard not to look directly at him. She also tried very hard not to let her imagination interpret his strange behaviour, not to let her yearning for him create some false scenario. 'I've never approved of brute force. It never gets anyone anywhere.'

'You mean you approve of him walking out on you because I told him to?'

'Henry would have stayed,' she said defensively, a statement which she knew sounded heroic enough, but which teetered on the brink of falsehood. 'I suggested he leave because I didn't want a scene.'

'Very wise of you.'

'Now, what I want to know is precisely what you want to chat to me about. If you have something to say, why didn't you say it yesterday?' You had every opportunity in the world, she thought, what with being supine on a bed with a suspect back.

'I was building up to it,' James told her, looking away so that she couldn't see the expression in his eyes.

'And what about your back?'

'What about it?' he muttered in a challenging voice.

'When I saw you this morning you claimed that you

were still in too much pain to even contemplate leaving my flat.' Her voice was acid. 'Miraculous recovery.'

'My back was always fine,' he said grudgingly, reddening, and Ellie stared at him, allowing this nugget of information to sink in.

'I don't understand,' she said eventually. 'Why the elaborate ruse? And please don't tell me that you were prepared to do anything for my company.'

Various thoughts which had been filtering through her head now congealed into one disagreeable one. Why hadn't she thought of it before? It all made perfect sense. She had ended their brief affair, but he wouldn't be able to let go, would he? Not a man like James Kellern. Not a man accustomed to getting his way with women.

So what had he done? He had dropped by her flat, legitimately with something from her father, and had then proceeded to feign some wretched back disorder so that he could elicit sympathy from her. No wonder he hadn't wanted her to examine him. No wonder the mere mention of getting him to Casualty had been met with forceful rejection. The stab of disappointment she felt on arriving at this conclusion made her feel sick.

Had he thought that he would find his right moment and then persuade her to pick up where they had left off? Had he thought that her sympathy would be the first step to her surrender?

She shot him a withering look.

'I needed to talk to you,' he said uncomfortably. 'I couldn't think of any other way. I knew that if I just turned up here you wouldn't hear me out.'

'What a mind-reader.'

'I had to drop the pretence, though, when that man came through the door.' He challenged her to say anything to defend Henry, and she waited in polite silence for him to say what he had to say before she asked him to leave. She wondered how he would phrase his request for the renewal of their affair.

'Have you started seeing him again?' Had he ever asked a more difficult, life-changing question in his life before? He thought not. What if she said *yes*? His mind was already leaping ahead to its own conclusion. How would he deal with that? The prospect was so horrendous that for a moment his brain seemed to shut down temporarily.

'We meet now and again,' Ellie said. 'And frankly I'm mystified as to why you're interested. I only hope you won't begin your speeches on how unsuited we are to one another.'

'Are you sleeping with him? Have you resumed your love affair? You both had space from one another. Does that mean that you've restarted your relationship?' He fired the questions at her like bullets from a gun, low, piercing bullets that demanded answers without giving her pause for thought. *Answer me, damn you.*

'I'm not about to sleep with you, James,' Ellie said quietly, and his mouth tightened. 'I gather that's why you came here with your bottle of champagne and your little scheme with your back. It won't work. I wasn't interested in a brief romp in the hay then and I'm not interested in it now, so you've wasted your time. You don't have to know anything about Henry or what he means to me. That's irrelevant. It has nothing to do with how I feel about you.'

'It has everything to do with…everything,' James muttered, his usual calm self-assurance having deserted him. He felt hesitant, as though he were about to grope his way over treacherous ground, without any real clue as to where the landmines lay.

He glanced quickly over at her and sat forward, his fingers linked, his arms dangling loosely over his legs.

'I've been thinking, Ellie,' he began, searching her

face, which she kept as bland as she could. If he had something to say, she thought, then let him say it. She, for one, wasn't going to ease the way.

'Have you?' she asked, after a while.

'About us.'

'Really?' Here it comes, she thought. A touch of staged vulnerability preceding the powerful persuasion tactics. The vulnerability was a good touch. It might disarm another woman, but not her.

'I know that you and Henry aren't involved...in that way,' he said, with enough of a question behind the statement to inform her that what he said was basically reflecting what he wanted to believe. 'At least, I hope so,' he continued with rather more honesty. She could feel terra firma growing a little uncertain under her feet. 'Could you possibly,' he carried on, 'see your way clear to sitting a bit closer to me? I'm finding it hard enough making this speech without having to shout.' *Yes, I would beg for you, if I thought it would work. So this is what it feels like to be weak with love.*

'You weren't shouting,' she pointed out. 'It's not as though you need a megaphone to let yourself be heard.'

'Please.' It was dragged out of him.

'Oh, all right.' But she made sure that she didn't sit too close to him on the sofa. It was one thing being strong and determined, it was quite another when proximity threatened to bring down both. If she reached out, she could touch him, rekindle the affair the way he wanted and the way her body wanted. She sat on both hands and waited for him to continue.

'That's better,' he said, staring at her, and she gazed back at him blankly. 'If you could just smile...?' His fingers brushed her mouth and she started in alarm and desperation.

'If I wanted to smile, I would see you out of my flat

and switch on a sitcom on television. You have something to say and I'll listen.'

'I need you, Ellie.' He stroked her arm and her breath caught painfully in her throat. Where he touched left a trail of fire on her skin. It was the very reason she had wanted to keep her distance from him. She didn't need her body succumbing to physical persuasion.

'Is that why you came over to London?' she asked quietly. 'So that you could tell me that you *need* me?' Her voice sounded normal, controlled. It could have belonged to someone else, because her mind felt anything but controlled.

'I know what you're thinking.'

'And you're about to try and persuade me that I'm wrong.'

He looked at her intently, until she felt her mind beginning to flounder. She couldn't seem to think straight. Every thought zigzagged off in different directions.

'Tell me that you're not involved with Henry,' he demanded, but in a mild voice, and she shrugged obligingly.

'Okay. I'm not involved with Henry.'

James's eyes darkened. 'Is that the truth?'

'Sure.'

'I can find out easily enough,' he said, and she frowned.

'Really? How?'

He didn't answer. He leaned forward quickly, surprising her so that she didn't have time to flinch, and pulled her towards him. The action caught her unawares and her body fell against his. His warmth poured through her, filling her with a sense of longing all the stronger because she had been trying to deny it for what now seemed like years.

She gave a little struggle, which was pretty ineffective because of the angle of her body against his, and then his mouth met hers in a hungry, searching kiss, prising her lips apart. She felt his tongue against hers, moving heatedly, restlessly. When she tried to move her head aside, he clasped her chin with his hand and continued with his relentless exploration of her mouth. He had the giddy sensation of coming home. A place where he belonged.

'I won't let you go,' he moaned. The fact that she was no longer being kissed by him should have been her opportunity to come back with a snappy, withering retort, or at least make a violent effort to free herself, but she allowed her body to sag against his. The temptation to close her eyes and wind her fingers along his neck, against his collarbone, over the smooth planes of his chest was almost unbearable.

'I need you,' he whispered huskily. 'I want you, Ellie. I...'

For a moment, her heart had soared. She had thought that he was going to say something else; she had thought that he was going to tell her that he loved her. Bitterly, she wriggled against him and wondered if he had run out of words that meant the same as *needing* and *wanting*, synonyms for 'you turn me on'.

'I love you, Ellie.'

'I've already told you, James,' she said, panting in her attempt to extricate herself. 'I'm not interested in being your temporary sex object...' Her mind was busy chastising her for having expected more than he could ever give her.

'We're not talking about that!' His voice was hoarse, and she was startled, when their eyes locked, to see a glimmer of desperation in his. 'Did you hear me? Didn't you hear what I just said to you?'

'That you want me... James, I can't make that my only reason for—'

'I'm not talking about lust! *Love!* Don't you understand? I love you.'

'What?' She blinked, searching his face. Had she misheard? 'Love?'

'That's right.' He had never felt so exposed in his life, and yet never as willing to risk all in pursuit.

'You love me…?'

'I love you. How many more times shall I say it?' Just to speak the words was a release. For the first time in my life, he thought, all my cards are on the table. He felt curiously exhilarated and uncertain at the same time.

'You can't.' Ellie licked her lips, torn between wild hope and the possibility of despair. 'You're just saying that.' But her heart was beating fiercely and she could feel a treacherous thread of hope snaking through her, touching every corner. She didn't want to believe him. She knew that disappointment caused by shattered hopes was the worst disappointment to bear.

'Trust me!' He massaged her shoulders. 'I can't live without you. It's inconceivable. I want to wake up with you and go to sleep with you, by my side.' He buried his head against her neck and she wondered whether he could hear her heart hammering away inside her. If she listened carefully, she thought that she could hear it, loud and clear.

Very tentatively, she raised her hand to his head and let her fingers curl into his hair. She felt him shudder against her.

'But you never said…' she whispered.

'How was I to know that that was what I was feeling?' He lifted his head and looked at her, and she realised that it was a moment she would savour for the remainder of her days. A look of love—complete, naked love. 'How was I to know that this obsession I had for you was rooted in something I didn't believe in? I thought I'd learnt my lesson. I only realised after you'd gone that what I'd felt for my wife was nothing at all like what I felt for you.'

Ellie sighed blissfully and lay back against the sofa with her eyes half-closed. She wished that he would carry on talking in this vein for hours.

'I'm not made in the Henry mould,' James muttered, 'but if you let me have some time I can prove to you that you're everything to me.' His mind boggled with the implications of what he would do for this woman. This wonderful, enchanting, infuriating, outspoken, sexy woman.

'How much time?'

'Quite a number of years. Hopefully about sixty.'

Ellie laughed and she felt him relax against her and cast her a sidelong look.

'Oh, James.' She was still smiling. She stroked his hair and then reached up to kiss him, liking the way the touch of her mouth against his was enough to make his body tremble. 'James, you don't need to *prove* anything. I love you. Why on earth do you think I left? I couldn't stand the thought of becoming more and more emotionally involved with you when I thought that all you wanted from me was sex.'

James grinned, a slow smile that made him look ten years younger. He was drinking champagne for the first time, flying on wings somewhere high above the clouds, seeing paradise. 'So...' he said with a great deal of satisfaction. 'You love me. Well—' he held her close to him '—I'm appalled to hear that the sex just wasn't enough to keep you by my side.'

'Perhaps,' Ellie suggested, 'you're losing your touch.' She looked at him speculatively. 'You could always prove otherwise...?'

'I could, but a man has his pride. I'm afraid that now all this is out in the open I can't make love to you unless there's a promise of marriage. I don't want to feel used.'

Ellie laughed. She thought ahead, down the years to come. She thought of being with this man for the rest of her life, hearing his voice, seeing his face, sharing his laughter. Moving back home and having his children. She thought of perfect happiness.

'Well,' she said thoughtfully, 'I guess this means we'll just have to tie the knot.'

And four months later they did.

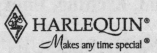

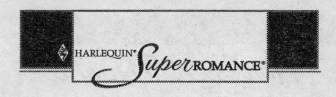

...there's more to the story!

Superromance.
A *big* satisfying read about unforgettable characters. Each month we offer *six* very different stories that range from family drama to adventure and mystery, from highly emotional stories to romantic comedies—and much more! Stories about people you'll believe in and care about. Stories too compelling to put down....

Our authors are among today's *best* romance writers. You'll find familiar names and talented newcomers. Many of them are award winners—and you'll see why!

If you want the biggest and best in romance fiction, you'll get it from Superromance!

Emotional, Exciting, Unexpected...

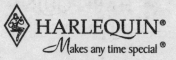

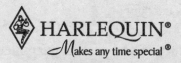